Blue Vegas

Blue Vegas

Stories

P Moss

Las Vegas, Nevada

Editor: Geoff Schumacher
Designer: Sue Campbell
Author Photo: Jesse Nabers
Publishing Coordinator: Stacey Fott

First Edition, Second Printing

Library of Congress Cataloging-in-Publication data
Moss, P
Blue Vegas : stories / P Moss ; edited by Geoff Schumacher.
148p. ; 19 cm.

ISBN: 1-935043-14-5
ISBN-13: 978-1935043-140

A collection of seventeen short stories all showing the seamier side of life in Las Vegas.
1. Las Vegas (Nev.)-Fiction. 2. Short stories, American–Nevada. I. Title.
813/.010832793/135 [Fic] dc 22 2009 2009933034

CITYLIFE
BOOKS
An imprint of Stephens Press, LLC
P.O. Box 1600 (89125-1600)
1111 West Bonanza Road
Las Vegas, Nevada 89106
(702) 387-5260
www.stephenspress.com
Printed in the United States of America

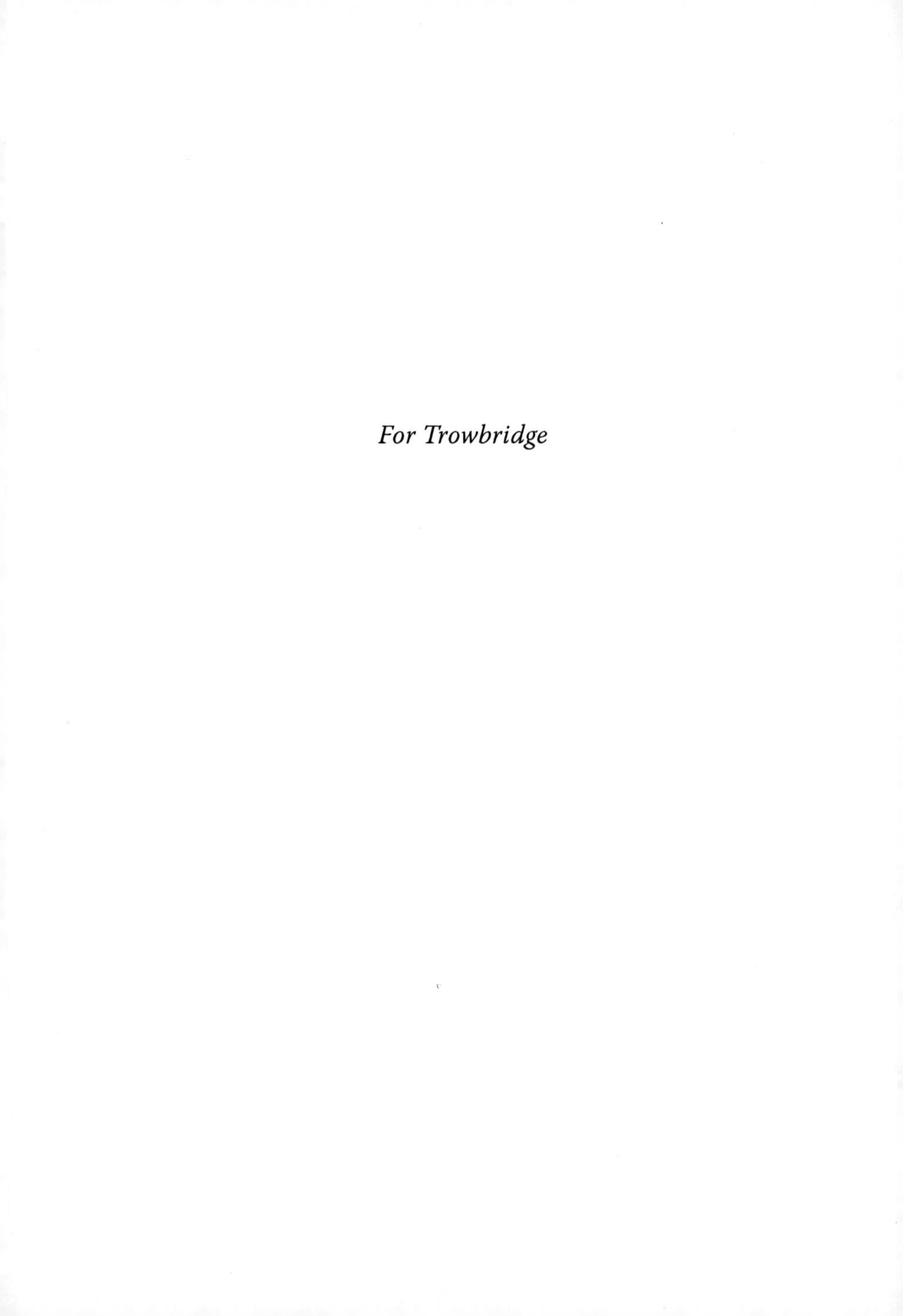

For Trowbridge

*Each sunrise in Las Vegas brings a dawn
of fresh opportunity which, when parlayed
with a little luck, can change one's life
in the blink of a moment.*

Contents

Performance Art

Two naked girls. One with blond hair, one with red. Face to face as they straddled a mechanical pony which had mercifully been put out to stud after a career swallowing quarters in front of a Wal-Mart. The pony bucked slowly up and down as the girls playfully fondled each other. Tits at attention as the crowd in the small barroom roared its approval. People stood on barstools, scaled the jukebox and video poker machines. Anything to get an unobstructed view of this opening act in what was to be the ultimate show of all shows.

The Rat Pack at the Sands. Monterey Pop. Beatles on the roof. All of it second-rate schlock compared with what was about to happen here. Performance art. The likes of which had not been witnessed in recorded history. Or perhaps never at all. How accurate could history books possibly be? Did some guy named Moses actually snap his fingers and part the Red Sea, or is it just a line he used to impress some cocktail waitress in the bar of the Mt. Sinai Holiday Inn? Suppose Caligula shared a bottle of wine with a girl at a café across from the Coliseum. After the waiter told his wife who told her sister who told her butcher who told his bookie who eventually wrote it down, it could have easily become indisputable historical fact that Caligula guzzled goat blood while watching his whore take it up the ass from a Christian, a lion and a three-legged priest. History provided few checks and balances to keep stories anywhere near the vicinity of the truth. But such was not to be the case in this swollen Las Vegas barroom. The print media pounded laptops while a camera crew from CNN set up near the small stage in the corner. The accounts of this night would not be skewed by gossip or spun by political agenda. History would be recorded accurately. A piece of history our civilization would not soon forget.

A midget in a duck costume knelt beneath the pony, his job to pump quarters into the coin box and keep the machine moving until this act reached its climax. Drunks howled with delight as the naked girls kissed.

"Suck the midget's dick!" shouted a boozed-up college kid.

"Respect the goddamn performance!" screamed a bulldyke, raising her fist in artistic solidarity to a gaggle of poets huddled near the cigarette machine. "And you can't use the word *midget*."

"I *am* a midget, you fucking moron," yelled the duck in self-defense. Wishing one of the girls would suck his dick.

This was an otherwise ordinary gin mill that tonight was destined to serve as host for a head-on collision between liberals and conservatives, artists and preachers, drunks and elitists. Where the biggest names in all of show biz willingly forfeited ego for the opportunity just to be among the opening acts. Although the best of the best was not enough to capture the attention of a crowd rabid to see the star attraction of this event, which would, before the night was over, exhaust all the superlatives.

Even the firestorm of the Stones jamming with Iggy Pop could not incite this restless crowd impatient to see the headliner. At the end of the bar an old hippie, E. William Tower, held court for the foreign press. A radical '60s lawyer, hailed decades ago on the cover of *Time* as a foremost champion of human rights, he was running short of causes in a society where most of his former co-conspirators were now SUV-driving Republicans. But one last chance to shine had fallen into the lap of E. William Tower when he discovered a loophole in Nevada law that helped him to secure an NEA grant to promote this ultimate show of all shows. The governor protested. Decrying the event by many names, none of them synonymous with performance art. But pulling the plug would have monkey wrenched a federal education appropriation earmarked for Nevada, and there was no way the Honorable Mr. Hizzoner would risk such political folly in an election year. So the governor protested only by his absence. But truth be known, he was watching at home on pay-per-view.

The star power of Bowie and Dylan sharing a microphone did not rate even a second thought before being cut short by *Ride of the Valkyries,* which now blasted from the Marshall stacks. Finally the main event was upon them and the crowd went batshit. Whipped into a frenzy as they caught sight of a short, enigmatic man waving in acknowledgment of the thunderous acclaim as security ushered him through the crush of punks, poets and clergy. Celebrities, academics and dimestore philosophers. Rumpots, regular joes and the just plain curious. Performance art. The ultimate human expression about to be staged for a lucky few. An event that would enthuse as well as repulse, because a man was about to die. Murdered legally by the state of Nevada as penalty for a murder he had committed four years before in this very bar.

Jeffrey Peck waved to the rabid crowd as he was helped onto the stage. Everyone in the room cheered him, whether it was to see him die, or protest the penalty he was about to pay for slashing the throat of the young woman who had ignored his advances. The newspapers, he felt, had ignored him too. His mugshot, the only photograph published, ran but a few times. A murder of passion in a public place deserved more attention. More respect for the daring of the deed. But like the woman who had stared up at him as her life seeped into the cracks of the barroom floor, the media could not ignore him in this, his hour of triumph.

The shackles were removed from his ankles as Peck was placed onto a reclining chair. His mind was remarkably clear. Transporting him back to his youth. A middle child who never received much attention. Shy. Scrawny with glasses. His awkwardness at sports leading to the pain of always being picked last when kids chose up sides on the playground. He withdrew to singular activities. Became bookish to a point until his short attention span turned him toward television. But watching only furthered his alienation as television tormented him with beautiful people doing exciting things amid a landscape of sex for the asking. Peck was a social leper in high school. Unable even to fit in with the nerds as he felt superior to them and thus them to him. He attended UNLV and earned a degree in accounting, a field of singular toil he felt would insulate him from the anguish of social intercourse.

He had no hobbies and spent much of his time fantasizing. But not traditional fantasies of threesomes with supermodels or winning the lottery. His private moments were consumed with dreams of things that most people conversely attempted to fantasize their way out of. He longed to drive in a carpool. To get stuck with a dinner check. But mostly it was for a wife to whom he could return home each evening and share the events of his day. And he thought he might have actually found that woman. Ten years younger than his age of thirty-four. Found her at work of all places.

Though the prosecutor claimed otherwise, Peck had not planned to kill her. He had followed her to the bar for a chance to stage a chance meeting, confident that once she got to know him socially she would like him. Not to mention that people who drank together in bars often went home together. She was attractive in an understated way that belied an inner beauty. An inner beauty confirmed for weeks after the murder by the newspapers and television. By the gallery of photographs accompanying stories of her life and the promising future that had been tragically cut short. All the while Peck was portrayed by a mugshot and single-word descriptions. Loner. Stalker. Animal. During the trial, he listened to the same flowery eulogies. A trial in which the jury seemed more interested in the prosecutor's tie than in the man on trial for his life. She had ignored him. The media had ignored him. The jury had ignored him. But on this night he was the most famous man in the world. And the most famous man in the world was impossible for anyone to ignore. Even Christ hadn't gone to his reward backed by the Rolling Stones playing "Sympathy for the Devil." Or maybe he had. Who knows for sure about history?

Artists, academics and drunks all screamed approval as Peck blew a kiss to the crowd, then leaned back in the reclining chair. The man who had suffered a lifetime in solitary suddenly found himself knee deep in friends. He smiled as the on-stage doctor prepared to administer the needle. Those few drops of poison that would seal his immortality to schoolchildren of generations future.

As the ultimate moment was upon them, recited verse rang from the crowd only to be drowned out by a riot of spirited opinion.

"Kill him!"

"He's a human being!"

"Bring back the pony girls!"

"Kill him! Kill him!"

"Lord have mercy on his soul!"

"His soul don't stand a Chinaman's chance!"

"You can't say *Chinaman*!"

Peck held his breath as the needle punctured a vein in the crook of his arm. It was only seconds before the crashing voices began to blur and images of life shot through his brain like kaleidoscopic buckshot as his senses simultaneously punched the gas. He felt a moving sensation. Like his head was rocking back and forth.

"Peck."

Back and forth.

"Peck. Come on. It's time."

Peck raised his head and slowly opened his eyes. The stark walls of his cramped quarters snapped him back to reality. The reality that he had indeed been transferred out of death row at the state prison in Ely. But not to a bar in Las Vegas. To the death house in Carson City.

It was time.

Those final few steps. A walk that often turned the most cold-blooded killer into a sniveling coward. But not Peck. For the first time in his life he was almost cocky as he was led toward a table in the room that had formerly been the gas chamber. The gallery would be crowded. All there to see him. His only regret that he would not see his picture on the front page of the morning paper. Not a mugshot this time. A photograph of him smiling as he bravely walked the proverbial thirteen steps.

His face fell as he entered the death chamber. No crowd. No people at all. Then he saw them. On the other side of a glass partition were but a few somber faces. Reporters, prison officials and his public defender, E. William Tower. Peck slumped his shoulders. Defeated. Offered no last words as they strapped him onto the table.

A curtain was lowered so the needles could be administered away from view of the witnesses. That was the final insult in a life littered with them. An insult Peck would not accept. There was no way he was going to die like he had lived. Alone and ignored. It would mean that he had killed the girl for nothing. But he had not killed her for nothing as he still possessed the power to earn the rightful recognition for what he had done. As the final lethal needle was injected, in an uncharacteristic show of strength, Peck played his trump card. Closed his eyes and focused his concentration back to the bar in Las Vegas where he commanded center stage amid the crowd cheering his name. His adrenaline proved an even match for the poison as he thought of people worldwide cheering in their living rooms as they watched him on pay-per-view.

In the death house the curtain was raised. Witnesses saw Peck strapped to the table, his eyes tightly shut to protect the fantasy. His mind began to stutter. Fading in and out of consciousness until his will was finally overpowered by the poison.

Jeffrey Peck died with a smile on his face. A fact the history books were likely to omit.

Clam Daddy

WHILE MOST OF THE BETTER TOPLESS ESTABLISHMENTS IN Las Vegas cloaked sexual fantasy in the sophistication of plush decor, flavored martinis and fine dining, the clam joints were more base. Totally nude with zero left to the imagination. Jerry found nothing sexy about a girl squatting over his face and cracking open a sideways window to her spleen. Yet there he was.

Jerry's face was lined too deeply for a man of forty-three. His tie was loose and his blue suit needed pressing. The music inside the club was loud. Unfamiliar. On the stage a naked girl swung upside down on a pole, while on couches and cushioned chairs dancers tickled their private flesh against the noses of strange men for twenty dollars a song, then lingered to tease up twenty more. Or however much they could gouge for ambiguous promises in the private VIP room. These girls weren't selling sex. Well, some were. But most were trading a commodity far more intimate, which started with a smile. Maybe a compliment. Then in the blink of a moment nipples would be brushing against the sucker's face. Bare snatch grinding his crotch. Those few minutes could make even the most pathetic loser feel like a somebody. Men thought they came to places like this for sex, or the illusion of sex. But in reality, they all came for that one thing that all too often eluded their daily routine. The chance to feel special. A feeling they could still hold close even after walking out of the club back to a bitch wife or a dead-end job.

Jerry watched as on stage the pole dancer now squatted spread eagle, whiffing distance from the hornballs seated ringside. Tourists and frat boys. Attorneys and plumbers. All leaned closer as the dancer reached two fingers between her legs and flashed the pink of her clam with the same wink of innocent flirtation as a coed revealing her thigh on a '50s cheesecake calendar. They may have differed in hair, height and tattoos, but to Jerry the dancers all looked alike. They moved alike. Had the same base wretchedness as all women, only here it was not hidden behind proprieties such as dating and marriage. And then he saw her. A girl who looked out of place.

This girl was different from the rest, even as across the room she rubbed her naked flesh against the crotch of an overly eager kazoo salesman. Playfully pushed his hand back as he bent the rules and touched her, but not so defensive as to break the mood. In a room where most every dancer sported a rack from the same torpedo factory, this one was the girl next door. She was almost tall. Real tits pert with youth. Her long red hair had a bit of natural curl. Her face was pretty. Her smile genuine. She was *Playboy* in a room full of *Hustler* and Jerry could not take his eyes off her.

He watched as she flirted and did her thing. Visually stalked her. Trying to build up his nerve to approach her. Took it personally as she slithered free from her G-string and aroused a middle-aged tourist. Then another. And finally another who forked over enough green to take her into the VIP room. After about ten minutes she exited alone, then reacted as she caught Jerry staring at her from across the room. She put on a flimsy top and walked toward him. He began to perspire. More with each approaching step. Nervous. Wanted to run. But why? This was why he was there, wasn't it? They stood face to face.

"Hi, Daddy," she said through an uneasy smile. It was odd that a girl who bared her all to strangers could be embarrassed. She tried not to show it. No dice. "What are you doing here?"

"This was a mistake." His being there humiliated them both. He wanted to melt into the wallpaper. "I'm sorry. I shouldn't have come."

"It's just a job, Daddy. Please don't be embarrassed."

"It's not that." *Of course it was that.* But there was more. Something far more unsettling than seeing his naked nineteen-year-old daughter soliciting boners from strange men. "Could we go somewhere and sit down?"

He followed as she took his hand and led him to a sofa in a dark corner. Perspiration became sweat as he could smell the two naked blondes tag teaming a limo driver on the chair directly across from them. Jerry's rehearsed speech had been ambushed by anxiety. Apologetic words stumbled from his tongue. "You have to understand I wouldn't embarrass you like this, but it can't wait until morning."

She self-consciously folded her arms across the sheer fabric of her top. Worried about the magnitude of news that couldn't wait.

Jerry would not humiliate himself further by going into detail. He leaned back and took a breath. Struggled to find the right words. Realized there were no right words, then blurted, "I need $800."

Huge relief. She thought someone had died.

He was still sweating. "I need it now."

"Relax, Daddy. I'll give you the money."

Just like that. The answer he needed. But instead of breathing easy, it made him feel even worse as he realized what a pathetic loser he had become. All for a lousy $800. Was he now the child and she the parent?

As he watched his daughter walk past a bouncer and disappear behind a curtain, Jerry thought back to a time not that many years before. When she was six. He had held her securely in his arms after she had awakened crying during a thunderstorm. Told her that he would never let anything hurt her. The standard throwaway promise to a kid too young to know better. But Jerry had meant every word, and it turned out to have been the defining moment in their relationship. He worked hard over the years to be the best father he could be. He asked instead of told. Listened before he reacted. Soothed the pains of puberty and puppy love. Ever since that night when she was six he had spoken honestly to her as a person instead of talking down to her as a child. And she had loved him for it.

She loved him still. Loved him this night even more as now she was able to be there, no matter what the circumstance, for the man who had always been there for her. The man who had picked her up whenever she had fallen. The man who made certain she would grow up in a stable environment even after his own had been shattered by a sanctimonious ex-wife who believed that sucking off the lawn guy was not infidelity. Kind of like good Catholic girls taking it in the ass to retain their virginity.

Jerry had loved his wife. Been faithful and true to his marriage vows for twenty-two years. His reward? Exile to a furnished one-bedroom apartment while his ex-wife was now free to give her all to tradesmen in any part of the 2,800 square feet with a pool for which Jerry remained obligated to the mortgage company every month. Even in a community property state, her lawyer had stretched him past the limit. But for years Jerry had earned a good income as a casino executive and he managed to get by. Then came the recession, and Las Vegas tourism took a direct hit, as did many in the local work force. Jerry was a middle-management suit without a contract and this made him expendable.

Wall Street, the banks, Congress. There was no shortage of villains for the casinos to blame in the shtick they fed the press justifying across-the-board layoffs. But it was hard not to read between the lines as they pled poverty in one breath while grandstanding multibillion-dollar expansion projects with the next. After a while the local economy leaned toward recovery, but by then the layoffs were old news. Except to the people who were still out of work.

Jerry was too old. He was overqualified. He was a day late. The excuses were boilerplate. A lateral move was impossible. Even a downward move wasn't realistic as hotels were now hiring kids fresh out of business school for half Jerry's price. It was like pushing a rock up a hill. Unemployment compensation lasted only so long, and what he had managed to keep in the divorce he pissed away on luxury items like food and rent. All the while still obligated for 2,800 square feet with a pool.

Finally Jerry was offered a job as the live-in manager of an aging 96-room motel a couple of blocks off the Strip. Professionally beneath him, certainly. But he took it so he could eat while continuing to look. Eventually he stopped looking as he grew to like the job. It was easy. Location meant he didn't need the responsibility of a car. Not having to pay rent, the salary more than covered his monthly nut. And working for an absentee owner eliminated the corporate stress of having to look over his shoulder. After work he gorged himself at the casino buffets, enjoyed a few beers at the sports books and went to the movies. All within walking distance. Life was simplified. Life was good. He enjoyed playing video poker. And then he began to enjoy it too much.

The owner of the motel had the books audited every three months, and the accountant was coming in the morning. Two weeks early. Was it because Jerry had borrowed from the motel account to cover his gambling losses? No. But Jerry knew that if the $800 was not put back before breakfast, it would be.

What Jerry had done made him sick to his stomach. Unemployment, even prison would be preferable to the degradation he suffered having to beg money from his daughter. A daughter he had watched, just a year before, cheerleading at her high school football games. A daughter who, just a year before, had swooned over posters of teen idols on her bedroom walls. A daughter who now shaved her asshole to glom twenties off drooling conventioneers. Jerry certainly wasn't thrilled about it, though he had somehow managed to come to terms with the thought of her working there. What choice did he have? Just for a while to save some money, she had told him. Hey, most teenage strippers kept work a secret from their fathers (her mother thought she worked for the phone company). But father and daughter had always been close. A special bond. He appreciated her honesty, but having to actually see it for himself tore him apart as it would most any father. He hated himself for being in the position of having to come there. He hated himself for embarrassing his daughter by coming there. He hated himself.

As she came back into the room, it was obvious by the confidence of her walk that she loved her work. And why not? The attention she got was a real high. She wanted to hug her father. The man who had always made certain nothing would hurt her, yet now felt such hurt himself. Wanted to hold him securely in her arms as he had done for her when she was six. Wrong place. Wrong outfit. She pressed some folded bills into his hand. "I love you, Daddy."

Then he was gone.

Jerry walked past idle warehouses toward the lights of the Strip, struggling to come to terms with what he had just done. With what he had become. A pathetic loser, sponging off his kid. Maybe in the morning he would be able to look past the self-pity and realize that his daughter didn't see him that way at all.

Jerry had hit rock bottom. Maybe in the morning he would realize that it was the place from which all great comebacks were staged.

Maybe he wouldn't.

Career Moves

The Forum Shops. An upscale bazaar. Conjoined co-conspirator of Caesars Palace that was a Las Vegas tourist attraction in and of itself. Fire-spewing statuary, pricey boutiques, a smattering of high-profile restaurants. Most of them still turning tables, though the hour of customary luncheon had come and gone.

Darla was twenty-eight. Short beet-red hair stylishly cut. Sleek-framed black glasses gave her the desired look of neo-bohemian chic. She lingered over an iced latte in a trattoria that spilled into the mall like an indoor sidewalk cafe. Watched passing wives hell-bent on maxing out credit cards in retaliation for husbands who had jilted them for a blackjack table. Window-shopping locals. Tour groups and gawkers. Then one man in particular who checked out the window display of a splashy boutique. Maybe in his forties, but looked younger. Well groomed. Brown hair pomaded up and back. Not quite as tall as a showgirl, thin as a young Sinatra. It was Darla's job to take note of such detail. The pointed toe shoes, close-fitting gray slacks and two-tone shirt-jac. He was dressed stylishly for an afternoon of shopping, if it was 1960. Yet the man continued to look at the nouveau designs in the window. And, with pointed suspicion, Darla continued to look at the man. Documenting her surveillance into a voice recorder.

What Darla could not see was that the man, whose name was Patrick, was uninterested in the window display. That his gaze sliced between the mannequins, targeting a floppy-jowled Texan buying a dress for his girl. She being of the younger, surgically enhanced variety. Probably some wiggler who had danced for him the night before and was cashing in on an opportunity to tease up some extra gratitude. But Patrick had eyes only for the Texan, watching as he handed the salesperson an American Express card. All of a sudden Patrick was no longer interested. Looking instead at an Asian man laying out cash for a logo-exaggerated tie.

As the Asian exited the store, he stopped and aimed a camcorder at a big-titted blonde carrying a Victoria's Secret bag. Patrick positioned himself directly behind the distracted tourist, then made a "V" with his index and middle fingers and inserted the tips only slightly into the back pocket of his jeans. As the blonde closed in, the camcorder groped the curves that fleshed out her tight baby-doll T-shirt. Then at the exact moment she passed, Patrick bumped into the horny tourist while simultaneously jerking his wallet from his pocket and, in the same fluid motion, sliding it into the front pocket of his own slacks. "Pardon me." The words hung in the air as Patrick was already three steps into his getaway.

His move had been smooth. Taken barely a second. The mark's libido had had him so distracted that he hadn't noticed a thing. Not that he would have anyway. Patrick was that good. But Darla's eyes had been fixed upon Patrick at the precise moment he lifted the wallet, giving her a bird's-eye view of the crime as if it had been played for her in slow motion. She bolted from her table and jockeyed quickly through the restaurant and into the crowded mall, intercepting him as he reached the escalator.

A surprised Patrick stood face to face with Darla. One look into her eyes and he knew to beat it downstairs.

"Stop!"

At the bottom of the escalator Patrick scrambled into the men's room and locked himself inside a toilet stall. He removed $2,280 in cash from the Asian's wallet and padded his own bankroll. Wiped his fingerprints off the wallet with toilet paper. Then with credit cards, room key and a $500 casino chip still inside, he wrapped the wallet in the same toilet paper and buried it in the trash. Took a deep breath, then exited the men's room prepared to do some fast talking. Cautiously looked both ways. Nothing. The coast was clear. He stepped confidently out the door to the curb, got into a taxi and told the driver where to go. As the driver wrote the address on his trip sheet, the taxi door again opened and Darla climbed in.

Patrick kept hold of his composure. "This cab's taken."

Darla called up front with authority. "Drive!"

The driver punched the gas.

She looked at Patrick. "That tourist probably still doesn't know his wallet's gone."

Patrick continued to play it cool.

"Do you always work the Forum Shops? Or do you move around?"

Who was this woman? A cop? Mall security? The mark never knew what hit him. How did she? Patrick was clever, always careful. Worked tourist crowds. And yes, he did move around. Never the same place too often. Knew all security camera placements and where the blind spots were. Never fenced anything or took anything that could be traced back to him.

Darla looked out the window as the taxi zipped past the topless clubs on Industrial Road parallel to the Strip. "I was impressed by the way you used that blonde as a decoy."

So she had seen it go down. But why the small talk? What kind of cop was she? Patrick had never been arrested. And, as he saw it, he was not in danger of being arrested now because all he had on him was untraceable cash. All he ever walked with was untraceable cash. So why the cab ride? Was she trying to scare him? Shake him down? What was her angle? Whatever it was, he had no intention of leading her to his front door. He instructed the driver to drop him downtown.

The taxi rolled to a stop at the corner of Main Street and Fremont. Patrick paid the meter plus an extra twenty. "Take her back to Caesars."

Patrick got out and the taxi drove off. Little surprise that Darla stood on the sidewalk beside him. He turned his back to her and walked away. Past venerable downtown casinos that had become a poor relation to the monolithic fireball that was the Strip. Hotel renovation and urban renewal having served as nothing more than a kick in the nuts to the character of this once-proud epicenter of the explosion that had become Las Vegas.

Patrick had blown into town a generation earlier, not long before the city had deemed it necessary to vandalize these historically proud downtown blocks into a pedestrian mall shaded by a monstrous video screen. Dotted with kiosks hawking cheesy trinkets to mobs of incited hausfraus on the cut-rate excursion from anywhere and everywhere. Nevertheless, whenever Patrick stood on what used to be Fremont Street, he could see back to that time when gamblers and scufflers kibitzed outside the storefront sports books waiting for the opening betting lines to be posted. Was invigorated by the air of a time when all that mattered were cards and dice, booze and broads. When women drank gin, not light beer. When men wore slacks, not athletic shorts. When people with no money and all the money crowded craps tables to turn nothing into something and something into nothing. People whose sole purpose for being anywhere was to lay it all on the line. Fugitives from a back-alley road company of *Guys and Dolls.* Not herds of vapid flesh bused in every hour on the hour to gawk at a light show spectacular only in the sense that there is nothing like it in or around Wichita, Kansas.

Despite the blight of progress, downtown still possessed enough character to ignite Patrick's passion for that superior time of cards and dice, booze and broads. But today he could not see beyond the cappuccino carts and baby strollers. Today there was no vitality in the downtown air as this vexing conundrum shadowed him step for step. Who was this predator who hungered for a pound of his flesh? She followed him into Binion's.

Even though the winds of change blew strong, the casino still offered that welcoming vibe of old downtown. And to Patrick that spoke volumes. He passed the dice pit on his way to a barstool. Looked up at a televised simulcast of Santa Anita as the bartender urged his horse around the far turn, only to see him fade in the stretch. "Any winners today, Harry?"

The white-haired bartender shook his head. Fact was, if he ever did have a winning day he would probably drop dead. "Usual, Patrick?"

"Double."

"What about the girl?"

A hungry boa constrictor toying with her mouse. In no hurry to strike. Yet she would. When? How? Patrick was served a double scotch neat. Darla tested the bartender's patience by asking for three different microbrews before grudgingly taking a Heineken.

"Your name is Patrick." Her tone was superior.

Patrick was tired of the game. He flipped open his Zippo and lit a Camel, pleased that the smoke made her cough. "Either read me my rights or go bother someone else."

Darla laughed, then handed him a business card. *Darla Drakeford. Zen Garden Films.* "I'm a screenwriter. I wrote *The Virgin King.*"

"You want me to go see it? Is that why you're stalking me?"

The Virgin King had generated film festival buzz and made some noise at the box office. Shooting her script had gotten the director a three-picture studio deal. Darla, merely the writer, was hired to adapt a novel that had been optioned by a small independent production company. But financing fell through and the project died. She wrote two spec scripts, but each lacked the unique perspective of her first and no offers were forthcoming. A year passed. Two. No longer hot, her agent dropped her. A friend of a friend opened the door at Paramount for a pitch meeting scheduled for the following week. But writer's block had left Darla staring at a blank page. Not one germ of a bankable idea. And in a *what have you done for me lately* business, she was getting desperate. Knowing that if she didn't come up with something fresh and off-center by next week, her fifteen minutes of Hollywood opportunity were more than likely over.

Darla sipped her beer, smirking at the sight of Patrick winding his watch. "They make those with batteries now, you know."

"Either way it's 3:30."

"Is it *exactly* 3:30?" Darla looked at him evenly. Sizing him up. Wondered why a pickpocket would dress in a manner that invited attention. Wondered why someone looking for attention would be so antisocial. "A screenwriter is always on the lookout for a character that will knock Hollywood on its ass. From what I've seen so far, that character might be you."

"I thought creating interesting characters was a writer's job."

"Sometimes fact is more fascinating that fiction."

"You don't know anything about me."

"You smoke unfiltered cigarettes. A drink means scotch and dinner is probably a steak." It was the ability of a good writer to dissect a person's character. She studied his face. His eyes. The dated attire. Retraced their conversation. "You live in the past. You've probably convinced yourself of some reason to justify your dishonesty. You're impatient, presumptive and have a high opinion of yourself." Again the look of superiority. "Is that about right?"

"You make it sound like those are bad things."

Darla checked a text message. Noticed Patrick's curiosity with her phone. "A little more high tech than that rotary job you have at home?"

"My telephone is quite functional, thank you."

"Can it download movies?"

"It can make calls."

She frowned at his joke, then realized he wasn't joking. Tried to put him into keen perspective. "Do you even have cable?"

"It was cable television that caused the world to lose its definition by exposing us to all sorts of new styles and genres without the quality to sustain any of it."

"The world isn't black and white anymore, Patrick."

"There used to be one world heavyweight boxing champion. Now there are four. How can four be the best *one*?"

"Progress creates opportunity."

"While lowering standards and blurring the line between good and bad."

"Don't you understand that the gray area in between is what makes life interesting?"

Patrick motioned to the bartender for another drink. "When I first moved here I used to hang around the sports books and listen to old men tell stories about gamblers who would lose a million and be down to their last two bucks, but instead of blowing it on breakfast they'd put it on the pass line. About the wise guys who past-posted race books with late wire calls. About dice mechanics who cheated the house and card mechanics who cheated *for* the house. Back when a regular joe could rub elbows with the biggest stars while listening to Louis Prima for the price of a highball. When showgirls were yours for the asking . . . provided you knew how to ask."

Darla had quietly switched on the recorder in her purse, capturing in detail as Patrick recounted tales of Runyonesque characters who painted the town green at casinos long ago extinct. He stopped abruptly, realizing his narrative played right into Darla's hand. "The bottom line is that it was a time when everything was either hip or square. No gray area. This town has an aura which can't be imploded. A soul which will not stop inspiring no matter how many landmarks are bulldozed to make way for impotent monuments to greed. There will always be enough legend in the air to legitimize my living in that black-and-white Las Vegas."

In the movie business substance more often than not took a back seat to style, and Darla was now positive that the discovery of this dimensionally rich character who owned a lifestyle unique even to Las Vegas had given her that rare combination of both. Darla needed to get him to open up. She needed to understand the mechanics of his craft. His backstory. His desires and fears. But all she learned was that fame and fortune could never replace the high Patrick got from just being himself.

"Where's the kick in cashing a check? There's pride in every dollar I earn. Sleight of hand beating the tourist. Counting picture cards to beat the dealer. It's what makes the steaks taste so much juicier."

"Naive sentiment from a man who never cashed a big check."

"That virgin king you mentioned. How long did you have to stalk him before he gave up his privacy?"

"He liked the idea of being famous. And so will you. This movie is going to be the best thing that ever happened to you."

Wrong. His tenth Christmas was the best thing that ever happened to him. Patrick had been a normal kid. Traded baseball cards. Teased girls and played with matches. But after a while he began to find childhood boring. Incomplete. He grew distant both at school and at home. His parents feared the worst. But by that tenth Christmas it had become clear that his aberrant behavior was due to the simple fact that their fourth-grade son was bursting with teenage curiosity. Under the tree that year, G.I. Joe was given his discharge by a new platoon led by Mark Twain and Jack London. Patrick struggled with some of the big words, but reading those books confirmed his suspicion that there was indeed a world beyond the within-the-lines routine of his suburban neighborhood. And by fifteen he was inspired to seek out the challenges of that world.

He offered his thumb to the highway, a determined teenager absorbing life's lessons at their darkest and most arduous. He educated himself by studying human nature and America's melting pot culture. Bused tables at a deli in New York until he was old enough to drive a cab. In Chicago he drew suds in an Irish pub. In San Francisco's North Beach he schlepped spaghetti, while after hours shooting dice in the secret grottos beneath Chinatown. That gave him the bug.

Unlike so many others, Patrick had not arrived in Las Vegas with delusions of breaking the bank. He studied books about casino gambling and probabilities. Learned that although he would win and he would lose, with applied knowledge and discipline he could tweak the odds in his direction and maybe, just maybe, stay ahead of the game. He happened upon a magazine article about pickpockets. Became fascinated and consumed everything he could get his hands on about the subject. Yes, Patrick thought. His life would make an interesting story. But it was a story to tell grandchildren. Not one to be corkscrewed by Hollywood.

Darla's professional future hinged upon getting Patrick to open the door to the inner workings of his world. And she was scared, as it was a future in which Hollywood's hottest A-list directors soon would either be asking to see her latest script or asking her to show them a dessert menu. "Everyone is motivated by something. If it's not money it's sex. If it's not sex it's something else. What's it going to take? What do you want?"

"Did it ever occur to you that people who make their living outside the law aren't usually anxious to be in the spotlight?"

"I'll fictionalize your character."

A thin disguise that would most certainly expose him to every cop in Las Vegas with the price of a movie ticket. And Patrick could no more live in Cincinnati or Phoenix than he could live on the moon. He lit another cigarette. "You're a writer who can't write, so you try to steal my character with absolutely no remorse that you would ruin my life in the process. You adjust your moral compass to suit your needs. You're no better than the hippies who grew old and turned into the same hypocritical tyrants they rebelled against in the '60s."

"Those people changed the world."

"And now they're trying to change it back. Censorship. No smoking. No this and no that. Between the fascist Republicans and the intolerant liberals, as a society we're steamrolling toward the ultimate inversion. Where the government is free to do whatever it wants while taxpayers have to ask permission. It's exactly the sort of thing that leads to revolution."

"You're plagiarizing Ayn Rand."

"I'm paraphrasing. You're just like every other product of today's society, conditioned to accuse rather than understand. To attack rather than live and let live. You've got writer's block, so you try to rob me of my job so you can line your own pockets by selling a story about robbing people. That makes you no better than the hypocrites who want to legalize marijuana and then send you to jail for smoking a cigarette on your own front porch."

"Movie studios have a lot of money."

"I make a very comfortable living, thank you."

"I don't suppose you would want the police to find out how."

Patrick stiffened.

"Talent has very little to do with success in the film business. For every Oscar winner, there are a hundred others just as talented still waiting tables because they never caught a break. It's a fine line that separates the winners from the losers." She looked him dead in the eye. "A winner does whatever it takes to cross that line."

Patrick picked up the phone and slapped it into her hand. "The number is 911."

Patrick drained his drink, turned his back on her and walked to a craps table where he put $100 on the pass line. Pressed his bet when he won. Played the percentages. Caught a hot streak. The camaraderie of the table focused on him, the hot shooter. Numbers, come bets, hard ways for the boys. Every move paying off. It happened that way sometimes. He was so caught up in the action, he had temporarily forgotten about Darla. He looked to the bar and she was gone. He smiled to himself. When you're hot, you're hot.

Patrick again tossed the dice.

"Three craps," boomed the dealer. "Line away."

But after nine straight passes, what did Patrick care. He lit a cigarette, all of a sudden finding himself hungry for a steak. A thick *juicy* steak. He picked up his winnings and turned to leave. Not tremendously surprised to find Darla standing in his path.

She followed him to the cage where he cashed in his chips. Followed as he walked out of the casino onto what used to be Fremont Street. Shadowed him step for step as he sought deliverance to that Las Vegas unspoiled by progress. That time of cards and dice, booze and broads. Not cappuccino carts and screenwriters. There was no vitality in the downtown air as Patrick took flight through the mob of incited hausfraus on the cut-rate excursion from anywhere and everywhere.

The Chinaman

C*ALL THE CHINAMAN. LET'S GO SEE THE CHINAMAN.* FAMILIAR expressions referring to the man who for over fifty years had dished up the finest Chinese food in Las Vegas. Lucky 8 was the name of the restaurant where he cooked and his wife, Ana, served, a traditional Chinese dining room adorned with photographs of the greatest of the great posing with the man whose food was legend. The Chinaman with Dean Martin. The Chinaman with Bob Hope. With Elvis, Sammy and Sinatra. Framed restaurant reviews praised the secrets of the Chinaman's kitchen. But the great man was quick to say that he kept no secrets, only that it took the same amount of work to make food taste good as not. And it was this food that kept customers loyal for decades. Drew the newly burgeoning downtown art crowd. Even suburbanites made the drive, as once they had gotten a taste of the Chinaman's kitchen they could never again choke down corporate strip mall moo shu.

The Chinaman was slender. Hair still dark despite his advancing years. And he was nothing if not a man of routine. He awoke every day at noon to the plate of soft-boiled eggs and rice that Ana had waiting. He showered, dressed, then went to the restaurant to prepare for the evening ahead. Opened at six. Closed at midnight. Locked the door and sipped whiskey with old friends. Then it was home to kiss Ana goodnight, eat a dish of chocolate ice cream and retire to his favorite chair in front of the television where he would watch Charlie Chan movies until the morning paper arrived. He would read the sports section and local news, then go to bed and rest for the coming night.

This particular coming night business was especially good, and after closing the Chinaman routinely counted eight percent of the nightly sales and added it to the money he kept in a coffee can under the sink. Counted the money in the can twice to make certain there was enough. Enough to afford him the one stop he always made on his way home those nights when there was enough. He sipped whiskey with men he had known forever. Talked about politics, the weather and why Starbucks found it necessary to have three stores on every corner. About how Ana had grown tired from serving and deserved a rest. Then said goodnight and turned out the lights one last time. Without fanfare the Lucky 8 was suddenly closed for good and fifty years of routine had come to an abrupt end. The Chinaman was retiring.

As he did on those nights when there was enough money in the coffee can, he went to the Venetian to play blackjack. He wasn't necessarily fond of the Venetian, but it sat on the spot of the old Sands and he felt that brought him luck. He had a passion for blackjack and often boasted that his winnings had put two daughters through Stanford. And those winnings had. He just didn't count the losses.

He walked through the casino looking for a double-deck game where the chip tray wasn't too full. One without an Asian dealer as they were too mechanical to suit the Chinaman. He found a table where he felt comfortable and played ten dollars a hand, winning some and losing some. Then the dealer busted twice in a row and the Chinaman took a fat roll of bills from his pocket and set it on the green felt in front of him. "Money plays." He always played the same way. Ten dollars a hand until he felt lucky, then he would bet $8,000. Win or lose, he would leave.

The dealer counted the $8,000, then got the nod from the pit boss to stack the bills on the layout in front of the Chinaman and deal the cards. Seventeen for the Chinaman. Eight showing for the dealer. The Chinaman displayed no emotion as the dealer flipped over his hole card, which was also an eight, but inside his adrenaline pounded as months of nightly saving came down to the turn of one last card. A king. It was over as quickly as that. The Chinaman put his money back into his pocket and cashed his winnings at the cage. Then he walked to his car and one last time drove home to kiss his wife goodnight and eat chocolate ice cream in front of the television.

Retirement was normal for a man who had worked hard all his life, but the simple pleasures the Chinaman had for years enjoyed between work and sleep did not now fill all the hours of his day. Ana watched Charlie Chan movies with him because she thought it would make him happy. But she found no entertainment in Caucasian actors delivering cornball Chinese proverbs, so she went back to her own routine of doing whatever it was she did. She enjoyed her retirement. But the Chinaman was too set in his ways to expand upon his routine of ice cream and old movies, and by early afternoon was left with nothing to do but watch the clock until it was time to go to bed so he could wake up and do it all again. An unjust exodus for the man who for half a century had been revered for dishing up the finest Chinese food in the desert. Few, however, knew that the restaurant had never been his passion. Only the means to an end. His greatest personal pride came when he sat at a blackjack table, adrenaline pumping as he waited for that $8,000 turn of a card. In his mind, that's when he really became the Chinaman. And that's what he missed.

Sure he had money in the bank with which to gamble, but that wasn't the point. What he really missed was the routine of putting eight percent of the take into the coffee can. The thrill of each night getting him closer to that jolt of excitement he got from an $8,000 turn of a card. He realized that he was not ready to compromise with life just yet. He decided to reopen the restaurant.

It did not take long for word to get around that the Chinaman was back in the kitchen at the Lucky 8. Ana had earned the right to stay home and do whatever it was she did, so a younger woman was hired to do the leg work. Opening night saw familiar faces sharing tables with the downtown art crowd. Suburbanites made the drive. It was business as usual.

By midnight the last customers had gone. The great man sipped whiskey with his friends, said goodnight and locked the door. Counted the register. Counted it again and put eight percent of the take into the coffee can under the sink. He was one night closer to the excitement of that moment for which he lived. He smiled. He was again the Chinaman.

The Curse of Frank Sinatra

BETH SMASHED A LAMP AGAINST THE LIVING ROOM WALL, cursing the jagged pieces of porcelain as if they had betrayed her. Stewart sat on the sofa threading an eight-millimeter projector with a newly discovered home movie, amused by the crackhead logic of his little sister thinking she would discover bundles of $100 bills hidden inside a lamp.

Beth trashed closets and ripped up carpet, positive there was treasure hidden somewhere in their dead father's house. Convinced by the memory of that certain Christmas when they were kids, when their mother had secretly traded in the old man's Buick for a new one. Then like in the car ads on television, Christmas morning saw a shiny new sedan parked in the driveway wrapped in ribbon and bow. But unlike television, the old man created an ugly scene as he bullied the car dealer away from his family and managed to undo the deal. By noon the old Buick was back in the garage where the old man unscrewed the interior panel of the driver-side door, then blew out a tremendous sigh of relief. The $197,000 in cash was still there.

For decades the old man earned a middle-class living blowing his trumpet in showroom orchestras on the Las Vegas Strip. Raised his family in a modest beige stucco house just like every other beige stucco house on the block. So where did a working stiff get $197,000 in cash? That was the question their mother had asked. Good luck at the dice tables was his answer. Didn't want to raise a red flag with the IRS by putting it in the bank. After she died, the old man joined the country club and traveled annually to New Orleans and Newport for the jazz festivals. High living for a retired trumpet player, making his straight-laced thirty–year-old son certain the money had been long ago spent. But Beth was not so easily convinced. Her long blond hair and killer body had made it easy to tease up whatever drugs she wanted from the L.A. club kids who flocked in legion to Las Vegas every weekend. But too much was never enough and it wasn't long before she spiraled out of control, twice facing hard time for grand larceny. Avoiding prison required a pricy lawyer, and both times the old man had paid. Beth vowed to find his money if she had to vandalize the house to its foundation.

Stewart closed the curtains, then sat on the sofa and switched on the projector. A square of light flashed on the plaster wall, then the grainy black-and-white image of a big-haired brunette standing with a young man in a duded-up cowboy shirt. The film had no sound but the action was easy to follow. She kissed him. He was shy. She reached behind and unzipped her dress, which fell to the floor.

"It's just a fucking porno," Beth scoffed as she ripped the stuffing from the cushion of an easy chair.

"A porno Dad kept hidden under a floor board for maybe forty years. He must have had a reason."

So they watched the film, various items in the room identifying the scene as the Six Palms Motel. The brunette maneuvered the cowboy out of his clothes and kissed his chest. Worked her tongue south. Beth sat beside her brother as they saw the young cowboy's eyes roll back as the brunette went down on him in grainy black and white. As the camera changed position they caught a glimpse of three men in tuxedos standing at the end of the bed cheering the action with a bottle of Jack Daniel's.

"That's Sinatra!" Stewart called out. "That's Frank Sinatra!"

"You're nuts."

"Of course it's Sinatra. Why else would Dad have kept the film hidden all these years?" Stewart studied the face of the man next to him. "That's Peter Lawford."

"The Rat Pack?"

"Who's the third guy? The one behind Lawford." Stewart squinted, trying to squeeze focus from the grainy image, then the camera moved and caught the third man dead on.

"Teddy Maxx!" they called out in unison. There was no doubt.

Teddy Maxx was a baby-faced singer who had a couple of Top 40 hits in the early '60s. Instead of reinventing himself to compete in the far-out '70s, he decided to stick with the Las Vegas showrooms, which were still forking over big bucks to has-been crooners with name recognition.

Stewart was a freelance writer who in the past year had stepped himself up in class with a couple of features in *Esquire*. He was ambitious. Always on the lookout for that career-making story that would dominate front pages from here to everywhere and make his name as big as the people he wrote about. And there it was right in front of him. Flickering on the wall of the very living room in which he had grown up. A Rat Pack porno, served up on a silver platter with Teddy Maxx as the garnish. He and Beth both leaned forward on the sofa, focused on the naked brunette straddling the cowboy as he thrust powerfully inside her. Then watched as she took hold of a hunting knife concealed beneath the pillow and, in one graphically painful swipe, sliced the cowboy's cock off at the root.

Stewart and Beth were struck dumb with shock. No way was this sleight of hand or special effect. The mutilation was too vivid. The horror of the pain too excruciating. The camera caught glimpses of Sinatra, Lawford and Maxx. All visibly sickened as the brunette arched her back and grasped the severed flesh that was still hard inside her. She thrust it in and out several times, then put it in her mouth. Licking the flavor of sex as she now stood over the cowboy who laid helpless in a pool of his own blood, then put him out of his misery by slashing his throat. The Rat Pack porno had become a Rat Pack murder.

A square of light again bleached the wall as the film end flapped around the reel. Stewart stopped the projector.

Beth got up and opened the curtains. "Teddy Maxx has fame and money. What does a man like that fear losing the most?"

"His health."

"His reputation."

Stewart did not like the sound of where this was going.

"Where do you think Dad got all the money he was throwing around?"

"It's not possible."

"He was blackmailing Sinatra, Lawford. All of them."

"No way." Stewart was nothing if not pragmatic. "Nobody had balls big enough to blackmail Frank Sinatra. All those guys had major mob connections. A trumpet player like Dad wouldn't have lasted five seconds."

"But he did." Beth's greed was working overtime. "Sinatra and Lawford may be dead, but Teddy Maxx is very much alive."

"You plan to just knock on his door and tell him the meter's still running?"

"Why not?"

"Because he'll call the police."

"After paying off all these years? No chance. Besides, cops don't scare me."

"Because Dad bought you out of every jam."

"With money he got from Sinatra, Lawford and our new best friend Teddy Maxx." It was a slam dunk. She didn't understand his reluctance. "You afraid of getting rich?"

Afraid of getting rich without getting famous was more to the point. Stewart's plan was to sell a tabloid story to the highest bidder, then write a best seller and auction the movie rights. He wanted to meet with Maxx all right, but not for a shakedown. He wanted an interview. He called an editor at *Esquire* who called Teddy Maxx's agent. Two afternoons later, Stewart and Beth stood at the door of a sprawling '50s ranch-style house in an exclusive enclave a shout west of downtown.

The Scotch 80s. A neighborhood built on old money, in the only city in America where mid-century success could be defined as old money. A quiet neighborhood that made you forget you were in the desert, lush with greenery and sheltered by the shade of mature landscape. Homes large and architecturally pleasing. Individual with character. Diametrically opposite the beige stucco cookie cutter with the ripped-up floorboards in which Stewart and Beth had grown up.

It was April and the trees were near full bloom, cushioning against the noise pollution of bordering thoroughfares. The soothing perfume of honeysuckle wafted through the neighborhood, which still stood proud even after many of Las Vegas' first families had traded up to opulent golf course mansions in newly fabricated suburbs. Colossal displays of pomposity landscaped with sterile rock and dotted with saplings that figured as an 8/5 underdog that they would mature to provide shade for the next generation.

These new communities had status, but lacked the class and character of the Scotch 80s. Even the roof rats that had found their way to these new suburbs inside truckloads of transplanted palm trees were not in the same league as the football-sized vermin that had earlier colonized the Scotch 80s. Feasting on the fallen fruit of backyard pomegranate and apricot trees and rotted bits of gourmet delight culled from the trash. Fat and sassy amid the lush foliage, these rats were living large. An aspiration of the two people standing at Teddy Maxx's front door, though these rats each had a decidedly different agenda of how they were going to hit the jackpot.

A housekeeper showed Stewart and Beth into the den. Dark leather furniture and a stone fireplace that burned despite the early spring. Window to the pool. Oak-paneled walls adorned with framed memories of half a century in Las Vegas. Photographs of Maxx with movie stars and mobsters. Presidents and kings. Proclamations of gratitude from a dozen charities and community organizations.

Teddy Maxx energized the room with a show biz sincerity as he entered and shook Stewart's hand. "Stewart Crane. A pleasure to meet you," the singer smiled through teeth that were better than perfect. Hair dyed jet black and a silver medallion hanging from his neck. Cued by his agent to lay just the right compliment on the interviewer. "I absolutely loved that piece you did a few months back about hip hop on Wall Street."

"My sister, Beth. She's a big fan. I hope you don't mind that I brought her along."

Again the smile as Maxx checked out the clinging mini-dress under Beth's open biker jacket. He kissed her hand.

What a suck-up, Stewart thought as he sat opposite the man who clung to false hope in a town where dinosaurs in black tie had been long ago replaced by slick production shows and hot young stars of the moment. But it wasn't too far into their conversation that Stewart changed his opinion of Teddy Maxx, as beneath the veneer he found the singer to be a regular guy.

He clicked on his recorder and listened with fascination as Maxx reminisced about his early days on the Strip. Of how he was just a teenager when he opened for Danny Thomas at the Sands. For Jack Benny at the Flamingo. For Ernie Kovacs at the Tropicana. Lost his virginity to an aging but still sexy Marlene Dietrich in her suite at the Riviera, then a week later deflowered a young Ann-Margret in the rain on the fourth green of the Desert Inn Country Club.

Stewart was enrapt as he listened to Maxx paint an intimate portrait of a Las Vegas before his time, but he had not forgotten that he was there for a reason. "What do you know about a place called the Six Palms Motel?"

"Never heard of it."

"You made a snuff film there, you fucking pervert!" Beth had no patience for this tap dance. She removed a vial of cocaine from the pocket of her jacket and snuck a quick blast.

"Stewart Crane." Maxx leaned back in his chair, annoyed with himself for not figuring the shakedown angle sooner. "Son of that bloodsucker Davy Crane."

"Don't mean to interrupt," called the cheery voice of Bunny Maxx as she walked into the den. Pushing seventy. Still pretty with a happy smile. Red hair sprayed into place. "Can I get you folks some lemonade? I just made a pitcher for the kids."

Maxx looked out the window with pride at his grandchildren splashing in the pool. Even for all his show business accomplishments he had never put career ahead of family, and he and Bunny had a good life. Married forty-eight years and they were still in love. He stood up and offered to give her a hand.

A moment later Maxx returned alone with the lemonade and a plate of cookies. "People today can be pretty forgiving. Look at that Hugh Grant fellow. Caught in the act and all the public did was make him a movie star." He sat down. Took a sip of lemonade.

"It sure would be nice to be back working on the Strip. Maybe a good scandal is just what I need."

"We don't buy the bluff, old man." Beth's patience was wearing thin. "And besides, Hugh Grant didn't kill anybody."

"Neither did I."

Stewart was through wasting time as well. "You know we have the film. Let's have the story."

"The Six Palms was out near the end of the Strip across from McCarran Field. It was a whorehouse run by a fellow named Charlie Crane, your uncle, who pimped out teenagers fresh off the bus with the promise that he could get them jobs as showgirls. When they wanted out, he kept them in his stable by threatening to tell their families back home that they were prostitutes. He had hidden cameras in some of the rooms, which made it a slick blackmail set-up. He liked to film weird sex acts. Sometimes with celebrities."

"Like Sinatra and Lawford."

"Those guys were never out there."

"I've got them on film."

"That's the curse of Frank Sinatra. He got credit for everything, but he also got blamed for everything."

"He's on the film."

"Look closer. That was me with two guys from the orchestra at the Dunes. Top names like Frank had all the crazy broads they could handle at the hotel. He never went near a creep like Charlie Crane."

Stewart's story had lost the Rat Pack angle, but he still had Maxx. Tried to piece together the big picture. "How was our dad involved?"

"Your Uncle Charlie tried to blackmail a popular young singer with that film, but certain guys from Cleveland had an interest in my future so they dug him a hole in the desert."

"Fuck that!" Beth tapped some blow into the cap of the vial and snorted deeply into each nostril. "As long as we have the film, I'm not afraid of you or anybody else."

"That's exactly what your dad said. Even after Charlie was whacked, Davy had the balls to walk right up to me one night at the Sands and tell me the score. The Cleveland crew wanted to plant him next to Charlie, but I was worried that maybe he'd given the film to someone else to hold for him. He wasn't asking for a lot, so I paid. Years later, he even had the nerve to make me sponsor him for membership in the country club."

Beth pointed to the framed accolades that crowded the wall of Maxx's den, a straight-up challenge to the fading star who still had so much to lose. "You're gonna pay again. And this time it *will* be a lot."

Maxx looked out the window at his grandchildren playing in the pool. "Bunny and I have a good life. Don't underestimate how far I'd go to protect it."

"The only way you can do that is with cash."

Maxx looked at the recorder. At Stewart. "Didn't you explain to your sister that if you write this story, she'll have nothing to blackmail me with?"

Stewart needed to close this deal fast. "You're right about the public being forgiving. But that's only with people who are forthcoming, not looking for sympathy after they get caught. Let me write this story from your point of view and I guarantee you'll be back headlining on the Strip."

"By telling the world you're a pervert." Beth was not about to let her brother double cross her out of the inheritance to which she was entitled. "You want those kids out there to know what a sick fuck their grandfather is? I want a million dollars! Now and in cash! And a hundred grand every month 'til you die!"

"Your dad never asked for that kind of money."

"And he died broke. I want cash. Now."

Maxx looked at Stewart. "Is that what you say?"

"Pay her or don't pay her. I'm going to write this story either way."

Contention hit the brakes as they heard footsteps coming down the hall. It was Bunny. She walked into the den and handed her husband the film shot so many years ago at the Six Palms Motel.

Maxx unwound a couple feet of film and held it up to the window, confirming it to be the genuine article. "I figured that if you two amateurs had this, odds were it was somewhere in Davy Crane's house. Bunny made one call. The boys found it in five minutes."

Stewart glanced at his recorder. "It doesn't matter. I've got all I need right here."

"There's no sound on this film, but you can still feel the chilling terror of the cowboy's screams as the sharp steel slices through his flesh." Maxx stood over Stewart, eyes glaring black with hate at the man who threatened to take away all he held dear. "You write one word and I guarantee you'll spend the rest of your life pissing through a tube."

Stewart ejected the flashdrive from his recorder.

Beth was terrified as she knew that this time it was no bluff. In fear for her life she tried to back away but Maxx slammed her hard against the wall. Pinned her wrists to the oak, his blood cold as he leaned his face against hers. "And mutilation is a walk in the park compared to the obscenity the boys will inflict on you. They'll chain you up like an animal and violate that hot little body in ways more disgusting than you could ever imagine. So vile and hideous that you'll be begging for a bullet in the head."

Beth struggled to get away, but no matter how hard she fought could not free herself. She raised her leg and tried to knee him in the balls, but the unrelenting Maxx grabbed her face like a melon and smashed her skull against the wall. Dazed and defenseless, she prayed for the knockout punch that would end her horror.

But the man whose life she had threatened to ruin was satisfied that his message had been delivered. He backed off and allowed Beth to escape his grasp. Rubber legged she fell to the floor, then quickly scrambled to her feet and ran out the door, her brother right behind her.

Teddy Maxx tossed the film and the flashdrive onto the fire, then put his arm around his wife of forty-eight years and walked out to the pool. Tossed a beach ball to his youngest grandson. He and Bunny had a good life.

Me and My Dad

KEVIN WAS FIVE YEARS OLD WHEN HE WATCHED HIS DAD PUT a bullet through the television at the old Hollywood Sports Book. It was 1977. No plasma screens. No satellite or cable. Just a tired RCA with rabbit ears tuned to college basketball on Channel 3. Where a missed free throw with one second on the clock had just turned his dad's $5,500 ticket on the home team into a square of toilet paper. Kevin did not hear any new words among the string of obscenities screamed at his dad by the man behind the counter. Nor was he surprised that they got kicked out only until after lunch, as even at five he had been around long enough to know that the management was not about to give a hysterectomy to a goose that laid golden eggs.

Kevin's parents never fought about money. His dad was a degenerate gambler and his mom was a keno runner at the Silver Slipper who reinvested her tips on the fly, so there was never any money to fight about. But that didn't prevent late-night visits from bent-nosed men demanding some. Most of his dad's friends at the sports books drove Cadillacs and flashed big bankrolls. Kevin could never understand how these guys could eat at Caesars every night, while his dad had to keep moving the family because it was cheaper to pay the advance on a new apartment than back rent on the old one. Springing for luxuries like bicycles and summer camp was out of the question to a man who kited checks and sold things that were not his to stay in action. Even when his dad did win a big game he let the winnings ride rather than lay a few bucks on the grocer. Dinner was often cereal or potato chips unless his mom brought home leftovers she snuck into her purse at the employee dining room.

Kevin's parents were losers and he had no respect for either of them. Not because of what they did, but because they were not smart enough to do it well. When Kevin was ten he asked his dad why they stayed in Las Vegas rather than move to another city where shylocks wouldn't bang on the door at all hours threatening to break his knees. The answer was so simple it made sense even to a ten-year-old. Las Vegas was the one place on Earth where no matter how big a hole you dug yourself, you could get flush with just one pull of a handle. One keno ticket. One parlay. No matter how much trouble you were in, each morning in Las Vegas was a fresh opportunity that could change your life in the blink of a moment. No other place could make that claim. Kevin understood it, but wanted no part of it. When he was old enough to live on his own, it would be a life far away from gambling and far away from Las Vegas.

Kevin stuck around to finish high school, only to see if his parents would notice, then moved to Chicago for the simple reason that it was not Las Vegas. At first he liked it, finding the people friendly and the winters invigorating. He enjoyed the lakeshore. Deep-dish pizza and barbecuing in the back yard. But beyond that he was not stimulated by anything. His life lacked excitement and his routine grew tired as he bounced from job to job, accomplishing little more than lining the pocket of his landlord.

His dad dropped dead in the sports book at the Mirage while standing in line to cash a longshot Super Bowl parlay. His mom grabbed the ticket before he hit the floor. She blew the money in an hour. A year later she cashed in again, this time in the form of an aging sugar daddy who moved her to Florida. Meanwhile, Kevin was now in his thirties. Selling washing machines and married to a woman who bored the shit out of him. He began to hang out a lot at the sports bar across the street from his work, a routine that would spawn inspiration.

People in Chicago lived and died with the Bears, Bulls and Blackhawks. Cubs or Sox. And everybody bet. Whether it was with a neighborhood bookmaker, an office pool or just for a beer, these people got more excitement sitting in a bar watching one ballgame than Kevin had felt in a lifetime. And it made him wonder. These people all bet, yet they led normal lives. Went to work every day, paid the rent and even had a hot meal on the table for their kids. He thought back to the guys his dad used to hang out with. The guys with the bankrolls. Who drove Cadillacs and ate at Caesars. Kevin had been so emotionally scorched by his dad's hellish world that it never occurred to him that not all gamblers were losers. That some were winners. Big winners. Kevin had been given a firsthand education in how to lose. Shouldn't reversing that knowledge be a formula for winning? And wouldn't winning be the stimulus he needed to kick-start his life? As he saw it, he had nothing to lose by trying to find out.

Kevin saved some money, left his wife and moved back to the place from which he had once escaped. He rented an apartment near the Las Vegas Strip and got a job as a cab driver.

Looked up his dad's friends and picked their brains. Hung out at the Gambler's Book Shop and studied all the recommended texts. Learned the intricacies of handicapping, money management and shopping different sports books for the most favorable line. Understood the need to stay focused on the big picture and not look for a quick score.

Kevin took a businesslike approach to sports betting, concentrating mostly on college football and college basketball because that's where a sharp handicapper was most likely to find an edge. In preparation for the coming football season he analyzed depth charts and scouting reports. Calculated the value of Iowa State having five returning offensive linemen and the potential liability of Bowling Green having only two. Developed mathematical power ratings designed to keep him one step ahead of the odds-makers. He quit his sixty-hour-a-week driving job because he needed that sixty hours for due diligence to handicap games. He was confident. He was ready.

Kevin's philosophy was that, provided each bet was for the same amount, all he had to do was win more games than he lost and he could grind out a good living. And it worked. By season's end Kevin had won over sixty percent of his games and owned the sweet revenge of succeeding at that which his father had so miserably failed. And this early success was not squandered on Cadillacs or dinners. Kevin remained conservative, saving for the two things he now wanted most out of life: the security of a paid-for house and a bankroll to stay in action. The next season he remained successful, putting these things within his reach.

Kevin was energized by the action. The thrill of winning. But he continued to stay focused, treating sports betting like the business it is and grinding out his profit. Then he had a couple of losing weeks in a row. Nothing to really worry about as they were *bad beat* games lost on a late fumble or a bad call. Sports book veterans would say that out of one hundred games bet against the point spread you will lose twenty-five that you should have won, and win twenty-five that you should have lost. Just luck and nothing you could do about it. Top handicappers would win forty of the remaining fifty, grinding out their profit. That was why Kevin did not worry.

But the next week he won only two of thirteen and did begin to worry. The following week he increased the size of his bets, something any pro might do when he is winning but never when he is losing. And Kevin continued losing, dropping all nine games. The week after that he ignored the sixty hours of due diligence and bet emotionally. Staggered his action, betting more on some teams than others. He won eight of twelve and lost $9,000.

Kevin was now in a full-blown panic. His house fund was gone and he hadn't paid rent in two months. He did not have enough cash to both stay in action and keep a roof over his head. But if he bet everything he had on one game, he would. It was the sort of irrational move his dad would have made, but Kevin knew he was smarter than his dad. Would win the game, then go back to the businesslike approach of grinding out his profit.

Kevin stressed all week trying to decide on the team upon which he would risk it all, narrowing his choices to the Raiders and the Steelers. He chose the Steelers plus six and a half at the Giants. It was an NFL Sunday and the downtown sports books were packed. As game time neared, Kevin checked out the Golden Nugget, Four Queens, Fremont, Plaza and Las Vegas Club. Trying to increase his odds of winning by shopping for a plus seven he did not find. So he went back to the Golden Nugget and bet everything he had in the world on the Steelers plus six and a half points. If he won he would be able to pay his rent and have a modest bankroll to keep him in action.

The Steelers were ahead by ten points in the fourth quarter and it seemed there was no way Kevin could lose, yet he had been losing games like this for weeks. The Giants scored and he began to perspire. With less than a minute to play the Giants scored again to take a four-point lead. Even though Kevin was still safe at plus six and a half, he broke out into a sweat, his guts twisted into knots as he considered all the potential bad beats that could turn this winner into a loser. Then, as if watching the unfolding of a self-fulfilling prophecy, his team fumbled deep in its own end and Kevin feared every gambler's worst nightmare. That the Giants would kick a field goal and he would lose by half a point. If only he had found a plus seven. But they would not kick the field goal. The quarterback took a knee and ran out the clock. Kevin was a winner.

He had a bankroll. Had rent. Still sweating, he ducked out the side door, invigorated by a crisp wind that spanked his face like that first Chicago winter. He sat on the curb in front of a pawn shop, not realizing the storefront was the site of the old Hollywood Sports Book. He looked down the block and noticed a cab driver unloading luggage, giving Kevin pause to consider the notion of betting the entire seven grand in his pocket on the Raiders in the late game. Which would, if he won, assure continued sanctuary from the work force by means of a more proper bankroll.

The longer Kevin looked at the cab driver lugging suitcases, the more he liked the Raiders getting points at home. He got up and walked back to the Golden Nugget to once again bet every dollar he had in the world. This time with a fresh confidence, backed by the knowledge that it was cheaper to pay the advance on a new apartment than back rent on the old one. And that no matter how big a hole he dug himself, he could get flush with just one pull of a handle. One keno ticket. One parlay. That no matter how much trouble he was in, each morning in Las Vegas presented him with a fresh opportunity that could change his life in the blink of a moment.

Plastic Jesus

GLADYS SURFED THE CABLE CHANNELS, SEARCHING FOR A certain toilet paper commercial she liked in which a kitten chased a Rottweiler. Twice through the loop with no success, she settled for dancing mayonnaise jars, then leaned back in her recliner. Gladys loved commercials. The way people with short attention spans preferred magazines to books. She was in her seventies and looked every minute of it with a platinum Eva Gabor wig, pince-nez glasses and capri slacks ruptured at the waist. But back in the day Gladys had been a knockout. A showgirl who dated high-rollers in exchange for expensive gifts and $100 chips with which to gamble, until eventually she lost her looks and went broke. Gladys had no family and her apartment was payment for managing sixteen units designed with asymmetrical space-age lines which, back in the day, like the landlady, had seen their share of high Vegas living.

"Hey, good lookin'. What's new on TV?" called Charlie as he stuck his head inside her opened door as he always did on his way home from work. Charlie was thin and tan. Once the lead dancer in a stage production at the original MGM Grand, he was now a room service waiter at the new MGM Grand. Charlie and Gladys had both thrived in the fast lane of a Las Vegas long ago, and they took delight in resurrecting the memories. He would titter about the showboys at Liberace's piano lounge. She often boasted of an affair with Elvis. Although once, tripped up by a third glass of holiday wine, she confessed it was just a quick blow job backstage at the International. But as much as Charlie enjoyed visiting Gladys, he had never adjusted to that creeped-out feeling he got from being stared at by a battalion of plastic Jesuses standing sentry throughout the cluttered apartment.

As it was with a lot of senior citizens trapped behind the economic eight-ball, chasing the ever-elusive progressive slot jackpot provided Gladys her only hope of salvation. Until eventually, as do many people with no hope, she grasped at a salvation she could easily own. Religion. But faith, no matter how strong, would not pick up the tab for a night on the town. Gladys enjoyed short visits with passing neighbors, repaying the kindness by doing small favors and baking on their birthdays. But she had little else and long ago resigned herself to the recliner. No purpose to her life. No reason to get up in the morning. Every day was like every other and she was merely existing.

"Before you go upstairs, will you be a dear and change the bulb over my sink?" Gladys asked without looking away from the television.

Charlie walked toward the kitchen, then turned on a dime as he smelled a familiar parlay of B.O. and bourbon. He opened a closet door and looked down at his neighbor, Wilson Jacks, a wild-haired man in his late twenties who cowered in terror on the floor. In Wilson's hand were four pills, each a different color. He washed them down with a greedy swallow from a bottle of Jim Beam. "I'm not going back upstairs. No way she can make me."

"Midgets again?"

"They're swinging from the coat hangers!" Fright had given Wilson's speech a jerky rhythm. "I'm scared, Charlie. Make her call the exterminator to come and spray my apartment."

Wilson was a big man who had grown fat from inactivity, and personal hygiene was at best a memory. He had been an aviation mechanic. A good one. Worked his way up the enlisted ranks at Nellis Air Force Base just outside Las Vegas, a career cut short when he was injured by a hydraulics malfunction. Broken bones had healed, but a severe concussion had knocked loose a couple of screws, which a corps of military head shrinkers had been unable to rethread. They were, however, successful in making Wilson dependent on a half-dozen prescribed narcotics. An assembly-line misdiagnosis justified by the disability check that appeared in his mailbox every month.

"I'LL KILL MYSELF!" Wilson shouted, jerked alive with inspiration as he climbed to his feet. "Never have to see those fucking midget cocksuckers again."

"Language!" Gladys would not condone profanity in her presence.

"What's the point of living anyway?" Wilson lamented, punctuating it with a belch. He drained the last drops of Beam, then tossed the dead soldier into the kitchen trash beside Charlie, who stretched to unscrew the burned-out light bulb. Wilson opened a cabinet and rummaged around. Then another and another. He foraged behind the cleansers under the sink, snatching out a half-full bottle of bourbon. "Look at the working stiff who gets bitch-slapped twice a day by rush-hour traffic, then kicks over dead the day before his pension. His wife who can't even take a crap because a houseful of brats are screaming at her." Even during that rarest of moments when Wilson crossed paths with sobriety, he looked upon a birth certificate as an affidavit of indentured servitude. Slave to the landlord. Slave to the grocer. The ultimate irony of having to square accounts with the doctor in order to prolong this miserable enslavement. Wilson's round face reddened as he worked himself into a lather. "Are any of us actually living? All we're doing is waiting to die. So if I can get rid of those damn midgets by putting a bullet in my head, why shouldn't I? I'd be doing myself a favor."

For the first time Gladys turned away from the television. "Suicide is a sin."

"Only because a stiff can't toss into a collection plate."

"God forgive you, Wilson Jacks." Today was but a different slant on the usual argument. "You have to believe. God can't help unless you believe."

Wilson flipped the finger to a plastic Jesus, only to be confronted by a dozen more. He felt boxed in. Raised his voice in defense. "I *believe* that a billion Catholics starve while the Vatican sits on the world's most valuable art collection."

"Those treasures give inspiration."

Wilson glanced at the television. "Tell that to the kid with flies on his face who wants you to send him 73 cents a day." Wilson unscrewed the cap from the new bottle. "Face it, lady. No matter what baloney those racketeers at the church try to sell you, the fact is when it's over it's over. Everyone who's born goes out a loser. Whether you're a billionaire or a bum, you go out a loser just the same. So what's the point of living?"

"Children, if you're blessed." More than a hint of regret in Gladys' voice.

"You know who's got the right idea? Bees. Take the drone. Fucks the queen . . ."

"Language!"

"*Screws* the queen, then croaks. The perfect come and go. No more nine to five, then punches out with a smile on his face."

Gladys had been around this block before. What she saw was a confused young man crying for help, not looking for a line pass to the fire-and-brimstone buffet. "Lord have mercy on your soul, Wilson Jacks. And pity to the friends you'd leave behind."

"The only friends I have are the strippers shaking their asses over at Cheetahs."

"Until your money runs out. I'm talking about real friends. People God put on this earth to look after you."

Wilson glanced around the cluttered apartment. "Tell me, lady. Who looks after *you*? Who can *you* rely on when you're in a jam?" Wilson choked down a slug of bourbon. Eyes crazed with conviction. "Your own self, that's who. The only person who'll do anything without wanting something in return is you."

Charlie switched on the new bulb. "How many times has Gladys washed your sheets to keep you from sleeping in your own filth?"

"She'd throw my ass in the street if I was five seconds late with the rent." It was the bug-eyed rant of a man stupid with liquor. He flew into a rage, again blathering about the midgets. He paced. Grew loud. Out of control. Terrified by the anxiety and paranoia that tag-teamed his brain. A brain he screamed he would splatter all over the wall if Gladys didn't get the exterminator on the phone NOW. Wilson's eyes rolled back in his head. He staggered and crashed ass first onto the plastic-covered sofa then, clutching the bottle like a teddy bear, laid down and fell asleep.

Gladys eased the liquor from Wilson's grasp, screwed on the cap and hid the bottle behind some boxes on the closet shelf. She covered him with a blanket. Often it was Charlie who sat up nights, deflecting away Wilson's hallucinations. But tonight that task fell to Gladys. She felt good as her faith had given her much more than just a reason to live. It had given her purpose. That most glorious of all purposes. She went back to surfing for the toilet paper commercial with the kitten chasing the Rottweiler, beseeching in silent prayer that Wilson sleep through the night and that she wake to save his soul another day.

Snatched

SHE WAS TALL, BLOND AND PERFECT. BRUSHED THE HAIR away from her face so that Ben could see her mouth as she worked him toward the orgasm he would have already had, had he not come twice already. Without missing a beat she shifted her body, the scent of pussy tickling his nose. Shaved smooth and sweet as a Georgia peach, she lowered herself onto his tongue, leaving Ben lost between conflicting pleasures. Two trains on a collision course speeding toward that explosion that shook him violently until both his brain and body went limp. Then sleep. The unafflicted sleep of an average guy who just had sex with a showgirl.

The room was still dark as Ben awakened to the sound of her rifling through his jeans. But before he could react, tall, blond and perfect was through the apartment and out the door. SHIT! Yesterday was payday and, like a lot of Las Vegas working stiffs, Ben always spun the casino paycheck wheel for the chance to win a free something or other and had a few beers. It was his Friday night routine and that's where he had met her. He reached into the pocket of his jeans and with great surprise and relief found his bankroll. Counted it to see how much she had taken. Counted it again as there was more money than he remembered. Then why had she been in his pocket? Maybe she left him a note. Her telephone number. He tore all the pockets inside out. Nothing. He locked the front door and went back to bed.

In the morning Ben stood in the bathroom, analyzing the person who looked back at him in the mirror. Definitely not the same unremarkable man who every other morning slouched through a half-assed grooming routine in preparation for the anonymous grind that was his life. The man who faced Ben in the mirror seemed taller. More fit. He wet his hands and raked unruly brown hair off his forehead, making himself appear almost handsome. Unfolding the pink of that sweet Georgia peach had given him an unmistakable confidence. He was very pleased with the new Ben. In no hurry to brush the showgirl taste from his mouth.

Ben's Saturday routine usually began in the laundry room, but today he dropped his washables off at the fluff and fold on his way to the sports book at the Orleans where he tied four college basketball teams together in a longshot parlay. Then to a neighborhood bar where he watched his games on the big screen and won them all. He put a twenty into a video poker machine and cashed out aces for $800. Went to the mall and blew his video poker winnings on some new shirts and a pair of shoes that weren't sneakers. A pair of slacks that weren't jeans.

The next morning Ben relaxed with the Sunday paper. Did the crossword. Checked out the classifieds. A few months earlier he had lost his job in the marketing department at one of the Strip hotels, and now he sold time shares. Like most sales jobs the money could be good, but Ben had a degree in marketing and always saw himself one day pulling the promotional strings of a big casino. Maybe even owning a casino. He had the dream, but never the drive. Until now. Sex with a showgirl had given Ben a fresh confidence that, in a future ripe with possibility, he could now attain the unattainable. He checked out a headhunter website and found a couple of listings right up his alley. After a shower he would cash his winning basketball ticket, then go back to the mall and buy a suit. A suit that would make the right impression at a job interview.

At the Orleans coffee shop Ben worked his way through a plate of pork chow mein. Who said breakfast had to be eggs? Ben was through living his life between the lines and it felt great. He paid the check, over-tipped, then shot the shit for a while with a bartender friend before walking across the casino to the sports book. He stood in line until it was his turn, then handed his ticket across the counter for payment. But none was forthcoming. Only a tap on the shoulder. Ben turned to find himself surrounded by police.

Eight armed lawmen manhandled Ben out of the casino and shoved him hard into the back of a police car. What crime was so heinous that it took eight cops to make the arrest? Local news crews pointed cameras as the police car was admitted through the gate of the underground entrance to the Clark County Detention Center. Ben was taken to the booking area. Fingerprinted. Photographed. Stripped of his clothes and made to wear the standard-issue orange jumpsuit. Ben had never been in jail before and he was scared. Scared stiff as he did not have a clue why he was there.

Ben was handcuffed and transferred to a special ward reserved for violent offenders. Murderers and rapists yelled through the bars, demanding to know how many people the new guy had killed to rate a private cell. Ben was soon joined by two detectives. One was stocky and intimidating with a gray buzz cut and cop moustache. The other one younger with wire-framed glasses, almost bookish. But there was no mistaking the threat of his tone as he fired the first salvo of interrogation.

"Where's the money?"

"What money?"

"Don't be cute, you fuckin' piss-ant. The ransom money."

The media. The extra muscle. To Ben it was all beginning to make sense. A man named Hyman Rudolph owned the hotel where he used to work. His son Zach oversaw the marketing department, but he was a lot more interested in strippers and blow than in working. Was quick to take credit for the department's accomplishments, but when he screwed up it was the department that took the heat. Two weeks earlier Zach had been kidnapped at gunpoint outside a topless club. His father paid two million dollars to get him back.

"You hated Zach Rudolph."

"No."

"You held a grudge."

"No."

"Threatened to get even with him."

"No."

"Will you at least admit that you don't like him?"

"Of course I don't like him. When I was in the hospital he fired me for missing a deadline."

"And you had an argument. A loud argument in front of an office full of witnesses."

"So what?"

"You threatened to get even with him."

"That's not true."

"You hated Zach Rudolph and you got your revenge by kidnapping him and extorting two million dollars from the old man."

"I want to see a lawyer."

There was an awkward silence, then the older detective sat on the cot beside Ben and took a shot at playing the good cop. "You're going to prison, Benjamin. The only thing left to determine is how long. We're in a position to help you, but before we can do that you've got to tell us where the money is and who else was in on this with you."

Ben ignored him.

The detective unlocked the handcuffs, his voice calm as he tried to gain Ben's trust and coerce a confession. "You know we're gonna catch the other guys sooner or later, so why do twenty years when you can do ten?"

Ben rubbed his wrists to revive his circulation.

"Be smart, Benjamin. Let us help you and you'll still be young when you get out. But you've got to tell us now, because any deal we make goes away the minute a lawyer gets involved."

"Why pick on me? Zach Rudolph is an asshole. A hundred guys hate him worse than I ever could."

"Maybe so. But none of those hundred guys bet a four-team basketball parlay with marked bills from the ransom."

Ben had cashed his paycheck. How could he make these cops believe that the only other money he had before placing the bet was from a showgirl who had rewarded his swordsmanship by slipping a couple hundred into his pocket on her way out the door? Even he didn't believe it. Why should they?

Ben's life was unraveling as if someone had pulled a loose thread. He broke out in a cold sweat and cursed the chow mein that churned in his gut. He had a vicious headache and the detectives refused to give him anything for it, then left him alone in the cell. To wait for a public defender because he could not afford a savvy lawyer with the expertise to beat this bum rap, though he doubted even the best shyster in Lawyertown could get him out of the corner into which he was painted. Ben had told the truth and he would tell it again, his reward for honesty being a chance to trade his dreams for a future of ass fucking and government cheese. To which headhunter does a middle-aged man with prison on his resume go when he gets out?

Ben thought about the time his apartment was robbed and the police never came. Thought about the time he was beaten to a bloody pulp by a couple of skinheads after a concert. How three witnesses came forward and gave the police the skinheads' names and the license plate number of the car they drove away in. How after a week in the hospital, the officer in charge told Ben that he had a big caseload and did not have the time to drive all the way across town just to arrest a couple of battery suspects. And when Ben reacted with normal indignation and pressed the matter, he was told to go find a few more witnesses and call back. If Ben couldn't catch a break as a victim, what chance did he have when they thought he was a criminal?

Ben was again handcuffed, this time taken to an interrogation room where he met with his public defender. She was a well-meaning woman past forty whose briefcase was so crammed full of case files it would not latch. She wanted to know everything that had happened up until the time of his arrest. Was encouraging as she thought out loud of ways to use this information to his advantage, then her optimism popped like a balloon when it became clear that guilt or innocence would hinge solely upon trying to convince a jury of twelve rational men and women that a showgirl had paid Ben for sex. She told him that a plea bargain would be the best way to go, but that he would still have to give back the ransom money.

Ben was strip searched before leaving the interrogation room to make sure he had not taken any pencils or paper clips that might later be used as weapons. He was transferred back to his cell where he sat alone. No appetite for the tray of jailhouse nourishment that had been pushed through a slot in the bars. He smelled like yesterday in a place that smelled like last week. The handcuffs were off but Ben's head was still pounding. Locked in a cell. On a cot where he could not sleep. He had read somewhere that one way to determine a man's guilt or innocence was to watch him sleep. The innocent man tossed and turned while the guilty man slept like a baby. Was anyone watching him?

It was well past dawn when a guard unlocked the door of the cell. Ben thought it strange that he was not handcuffed as he was led out of the ward to his arraignment. Wondered what gems of encouragement his public defender would offer, or would she again advise him to plead guilty to lighten the weight of her briefcase? But Ben never saw her. The guard took him to the booking area, then left him in the property room where his clothes, wallet and keys were dumped out of a clear plastic bag.

As Ben signed for his belongings he was given no explanation. There were no detectives. No cops at all. Just the property clerk who read from a sheet of paper that his arraignment had been canceled and he was free to get dressed and go. What Ben would later read in the newspaper was that while he was locked up, one of the real kidnappers was arrested after he had gotten drunk and blown a wad of the ransom money on cold dice. Then, in exchange for a sentencing recommendation, he detailed the kidnapping plot masterminded by one of Ben's former co-workers to set him up as the patsy. The argument with Zach Rudolph gave Ben motive. His Friday night routine made him an easy mark for the hooker they hired to fuck him stupid and plant ransom cash in his jeans. The idea was that Ben would convict himself with an implausible story that no one would believe.

Twenty hours earlier Ben had been threatened with twenty years. Embarrassed, belittled and demoralized. Robbed of his future and raped of his dignity. Then without explanation or apology had been set free with just enough time to shower off the filth of degradation and get to his time share cubicle. But today Ben would not go to the cubicle. His headache gone and suddenly hungry, he stood tall as he walked down Main Street toward the diner at the Golden Gate where he would wrap himself around a hot plate of ham and eggs. Then he would go to the Orleans and demand his basketball winnings. Then to the mall where he would buy a suit that would make the right impression at a job interview. Ben once again held close the confidence that, in a future ripe with possibility, he could attain the unattainable. A confidence inspired by the scent of a showgirl. Shaved smooth and sweet as a Georgia peach.

Pastrami on Rye

George Greenbaum waited alone at a table in the casino deli. Cooled his throat with a sip of Dr. Brown's celery soda, silently cursing the new smoking law that denied him the pleasure of a cigar. He closed his menu, unsure why he had opened it in the first place as for almost sixty years his deli order had been the same. Pastrami and Swiss on rye with butter and mustard. The old Jews used to give him hell about the butter. Didn't belong. Blew the parlay. But who was left to give him hell? These days, finding a Jew behind a deli counter in Las Vegas was like pissing up a rope. Especially in the hotels, where inexperienced half-wits were hired on the basis that their applications happened to be on top of the pile. Every one of them a clueless schmuck who couldn't tell brisket from a bialy. Who couldn't make change without the register telling them how much.

George was bald and black-rimmed glasses framed his wilted face. He wore a short-sleeve white shirt. Loosened his tie and folded it into his trouser pocket, not wanting to prompt the question of where he had been. He was embarrassed. Bitter at the degradation of having to beg McDonald's for a job pouring coffee and wiping tables. Making seniors feel useful was what they called it. Castrated was how he had felt, seated across a table from the perky young girl who perused his application.

"Why'd you leave your last job?"

"For performing a common courtesy which I'm told is now politically incorrect."

"Was a lawsuit filed?"

"Some pinch-faced old crone couldn't take a compliment and Skippy with the pimples told me to turn in my apron. End of story."

"I see."

"No. You don't see."

She looked at the blank spaces on the employment history portion of his application. "Where'd you work before that?"

"I was in business."

"What kind of business?"

"What specific qualifications are required to wipe ketchup off tables?"

"Lots of seniors come to work here 'cause they miss being around people." She smacked her gum. Gave him an evaluating look. "You don't act like much of a people person."

"Doesn't anybody come to work here because they have rent to pay?"

And so it went. More inane interrogation sucker punching his pride until finally he was dismissed, and his application placed on the bottom of the pile.

George was from Pittsburgh. Grew up at the tail end of the Depression and started earning his keep when he was seven, shining shoes and running errands for the gamblers in the horse room behind his uncle's barber shop. By twenty he began booking ball games and quickly found himself faced with the usual problems of the trade. The toughest of which was that as a neighborhood independent, it was difficult for him to obtain a solid betting line that had not already been trampled upon by the opinions of connected bookmakers. Still, George managed to make a good living.

By the 1960s the sports books in Las Vegas were putting up the most solid betting lines in the country. They also had wire service tickers, similar to stock tickers, which provided sports news and scores. Not up to the minute, but as close as it got in those days. Connected bookmakers had access to this information, but the neighborhood independents did not and George saw opportunity. It was the winter of 1967 when he made deals with four Pittsburgh bookmakers, loaded his car and headed for a place where the weather wasn't quite so argumentative. Every week George went downtown to Western Union to collect four $250 money orders from Pittsburgh. In return, he called each bookmaker once a day with the opening point spreads from Churchill Downs, then the most respected of the sports books in Las Vegas.

He included injury reports and other pertinent data. It was illegal to telephone this information across state lines, but it was a thousand tax-free dollars a week for a few minutes work a day.

Ten years later George had clients in cities across the country, calling them several times each day, monitoring point spread movement and last-minute lineup changes. He was pocketing more than $200,000 a year just by dropping coins into a pay phone. Then the law changed. Point spreads were classified as news and could now be legally transmitted across state lines. They began to appear in newspapers, though the timeliness of betting lines printed the night before was of little use to bookmakers. Line services started to spring up everywhere, offering unlimited toll-free access to up-to-the-minute Las Vegas numbers at cut-rate prices. It wasn't long before George was out of business.

But life was good. He calculated that he had enough money to smoke cigars by the pool well into his nineties. Failing, however, to account for inflation and the countless other economic variables that could deteriorate a life savings into pocket lint. Investing the money would have left him many times a millionaire, but a man with no visible means of support could hardly have built a bank account or investment portfolio without the IRS climbing up his ass. So he squirreled away his cash in a safe deposit box. Each week he removed expense money, these days hoping that what little remained would last as long as he did. It would. If he didn't plan on living past Christmas.

Tom Thornton walked past a line of tourists waiting for tables. He was thirty-five and cocky. Blond hair freshly cut. Gold chain. Lakers jersey over cargo shorts. He knew George from the sports book at the Mirage and had invited him to lunch to explain the details of a sure thing he was going to let him in on.

Thornton laughed as he sat down. "What the hell are you made up for?"

George's short-sleeve dress shirt would have been cause for double take to any of the sports book denizens who had never seen him out of the matching blue track suit he wore every day to the Mirage. The minor detail of not having any money with which to bet wasn't going to stop him from kibitzing with regulars who were the closest thing he had to family. People on both sides of the counter who respected his pedigree as well as his opinion. None of whom knew he was broke. The sports book was the only place in the world where George felt alive.

Thornton renewed his boast that he had a sure thing.

"I've heard a lot of people say that in seventy-eight years. They all ended up broke or in the can."

"This can't miss. I did it last year and it's totally on the legit . . . I think."

George would hear him out. A free lunch was guarantee of that.

Over pastrami Thornton made his pitch, which centered on a certain pro football handicapping contest. Many of the casinos promoted them. No point spreads. Just pay a one-time entry fee of $25 and pick which NFL teams you think will win each weekend. A $30,000 prize if you picked the most weekly winners, $100,000 if you had the most wins at the end of the season. Needless to say, these contests were popular.

Thornton had put together a group of people who would submit multiple entries. Each week of the season he would take the four biggest favorites (since there was no point spread, these teams almost always won) and wheel them with the home *and* visiting teams on the rest of the schedule, thus covering almost every possible winning combination. One of the entries would likely take home at least a share of the weekly prize money.

"If you made a score last year, why do you need me?"

"One guy got greedy. I need partners I can trust. People at the Mirage know you for a lot of years as a stand-up guy."

"You can't possibly cover all the combinations. Besides, what if a favorite loses?"

"Some weeks one loss can grab the money. Especially if it's the same loss everybody else has."

"But it's not a sure thing."

"The NFL is a league of upsets. Which works in our favor because we cover both sides of every game. I'm telling you, George. This can't miss."

Uncovered combinations, upsets, greedy partners. Of course it could miss. Still, George liked the odds. Seeing it as a well-calculated plan with a great shot to pay off, affording him one final opportunity to reclaim his life.

Thornton kept pitching. Not aware that George was already sold. "Bottom line is, after the tax bite I take half of all the prize money. The other half gets divided equally between everybody in the group."

George could taste the long-overdue indulgence of five courses at Hugo's Cellar. He would treat himself to a box of Cuban cigars. Pay his rent a year in advance. His adrenaline rushed like a man whose last two bucks was on the nose of a longshot with a thirty-length lead in the stretch.

"I won't bore you with the math." Thornton took a bite of his sandwich. Spoke confidently as he chewed. "But last year everybody got back their $500 investment ten times over."

"*Investment*?" George's life flashed before his eyes. Forget fine dining and cigars. It was the rent. He had to have money for the rent. Maybe he had heard it wrong. Tom Thornton could not be so cruel as to throw a rope to a drowning man only to snatch it from his grasp. But then, Thornton didn't know that George was a drowning man. Yes, he must have heard wrong. "I thought you were putting up the money."

"My idea. I figure all the combinations. You guys come up with the stake." Thornton tossed his napkin onto the table. "You in?"

Five hundred. Might as well have been five million. And admitting poverty would have cast him in a different light at the sports book, the one place in the world where he retained his dignity. So George declined by reason that the scheme had flaws. A final kick in the nuts to a man already defeated by the realization that his life was over. That he was merely existing. And just barely.

Thornton got up. "If you change your mind, let me know. Season starts in two weeks."

George watched through tired eyes as a last chance to reclaim his life walked out of the deli and into the casino. The waitress asked if he wanted anything else, then left the check. He paid for pastrami and Swiss on rye with butter and mustard. For two.

Unconditionally

THE ART ON THE WALL WAS MONET. RATHER, WORKS THAT had been collected by Monet. Seventeenth-century Flemish armchairs with original tapestry flanked a square wrought-iron table from Depression-era Louisiana. The mantelpiece came from the English manor house where Edward VIII stole away for forbidden weekends with Wallis Simpson. Facing the fireplace, a red velvet settee from the court of Louis XIV. Even the most unobtrusive ashtray was precisely positioned in this room where eclecticism was matched by warmth and charm.

Amanda was an attractive woman. Quite beautiful actually. Her auburn hair was long with a slight natural curl. She admitted to thirty-five but had passed forty, a claim few would doubt as a daily regimen of skin care and exercise kept vibrant the weapons nature had given her. Amanda was in love. True and unconditional love. She had decorated this room herself. Inspired by her love which was to be forever, she tastefully fused the schematic clutter of mismatched antiques with the resplendent freshness of newly cut stems that were changed each morning. From the most petite Lalique bud vase to the centerpiece Japanese porcelain bowl, an energizing sweetness permeated the room. This day it was a delicate grouping of calla lilies and tulips the color of Roma tomatoes. Amanda stood by the window contemplating the water splashing from a mosaic fountain, then turned as she heard someone enter the room.

A tall, slender woman walked toward her. Her name was Jennifer. In her mid-twenties. She took off her coat to reveal jeans and a loose-fitting vest. Her face was fresh and vibrant, framed by shoulder-length vanilla hair that reacted to even her slightest movement.

Without a word, Jennifer raked back Amanda's hair and ran her tongue slowly up the side of her neck. Nibbling as she nestled behind her ear. Amanda's head rocked backward as she weakened with a desire evidenced by whimpers that could be felt if not heard. Her eyes still closed, she slid her hands beneath her lover's vest, which soon fell to the carpet. Jennifer unbuttoned Amanda's blouse and leaned forward, brushing their breasts together. In a moment they lay naked on centuries-old red velvet, fingers locked together as they kissed. Jennifer's tongue slowly circled Amanda's breasts. Gently biting them. Amanda tugged vanilla hair with both fists as she felt her nipple stiffen inside her lover's mouth.

Jennifer moaned as Amanda's fingers explored her soft inner crevices, then quickly pulled away. "Careful, baby. Your nails are sharp." Their flesh again pressed together. Moans of pleasure echoed each caress, then, "OW!" This time Jennifer screamed it, jerking her head in horror to see a chicken pecking at the inner curve of her ass.

She threw herself off of Amanda and onto the floor, feathers flying as the chicken squawked bloody murder, shot across the room and crashed into a sculpture of Shen Yang marble. Jennifer dove for cover behind a chair as a dozen more chickens zigzagged into the room. Naked and panic-stricken, she peeked over the chair and saw an old man dressed in a bathrobe with a six-gun on his hip. The man was very old. Almost hollow. Wore a ten-gallon hat and fuzzy slippers. He picked up the dazed bird and shuffled slowly toward the settee and sat beside Amanda.

"Sorry," the old man muttered. "I brought Bluebell in to watch *Matlock* and guess I forgot to shut the dang door."

Jennifer scrambled for her clothes and dressed quickly, then lost her balance and fell on her ass as squawking poultry pecked at her bare feet. Looked up in disbelief at the surreal portrait of her naked lover sitting on priceless red velvet beside a decaying cowboy in fuzzy slippers holding a chicken. She didn't know whether to scream or scram. She scrammed.

Most bored wives of privilege filled the void by having suitable sex with the golf pro or vile sex with the gardener. Amanda opted to spend her husband's money on the anonymous passion of high-end lesbian hookers. But it hadn't always been that way.

Stationed near Las Vegas during World War II, her husband stuck around after his discharge. Worked as a craps dealer in the sawdust joints on Fremont Street. Kept his vices in check and at the end of each week had a few dollars to put in the bank. Later, when the corporations muscled their way onto the Strip, a friend convinced him to take his money out of the bank and buy some casino stock. It proved a good investment and he bought some more. Years later he cashed out millions.

It was around that time he met Amanda. A damsel in distress who he helped escape a serious jam she had gotten into with a lowlife who preyed on young girls fresh off the bus. Amanda was grateful to have been given a second chance at life, eager to repay the old man's kindness the only way she knew how. But he would not take advantage of her vulnerability, saying only that he was happy to have been able to help. They developed a friendship that over time led to courtship. He supported her interests and treated her with a respect she had never known dating younger men. He was seventy-one and she was twenty-four and they shared a love which would be forever.

As the years passed and age started to rob him of his marbles, Amanda saw to all his needs. Indulged his eccentricities, of which keeping chickens in the house was not even close to being the most bizarre. She had sex with women because she could never be unfaithful with another man as long as he was alive. And probably not even after that. She loved him that much.

Amanda shooed poultry off seventeenth-century Flemish armchairs, then pushed back the old man's ten-gallon hat and kissed him tenderly on the forehead. "You and Bluebell go watch your show. I'll make us some popcorn and be right in."

Amanda helped the frail old cowboy to his feet and made sure Bluebell was secure in his arm. Then steadied him as he shuffled out of the room, the rest of the chickens following dutifully in a row.

This beautiful naked woman whose long auburn hair had a slight natural curl. This woman of desire who kept sexually vibrant the weapons nature had given her. This woman who could have had anyone went into the kitchen to make popcorn for a crackbrained old man and his pet chicken. Yes, she loved him that much. A love that would be forever.

The 8:16 to Nowheresville

SANDRA STOOD JUST OUT OF REACH OF THE LOOMING shadow cast by the green behemoth that was the MGM Grand, every few moments leaning impatiently off the curb in hopes of glimpsing her bus, which was, according to her watch, five minutes late. Hers was usually an air-conditioned commute, but today she had to get up an hour early and transfer twice on the Citizens Area Transit because her car was in the shop. Today skin would stick to her floral print dress as she punched the time clock, courtesy of the thermometer, which had already begun its ascent toward the forecast 112 degrees. Today was a work day destined to be as monotonous as every other work day. Answering phones at a downtown property management company. Sorting mail. Lying to pissed off tenants that the boss was not in. Making Sandra just another rat in a maze sniffing the false promise of cheese.

She had been first at the bus stop, but when the door pulled open, asses and elbows jostled her to the end of the line. Last to get on, she gagged on a whiff of street perfume steaming off a bum hunched next to the only empty seat. A bum who caught her in his manic gaze.

"Sandra? It's me, Bob. Bob Brewer."

Stunned, she looked down at the creature who spoke through the yellowish brown of rotting teeth. Whose jeans were stained and reeked of urine. This was certainly not how Sandra envisioned this moment she had waited for every day of the past twenty years.

She and Bob had been sweethearts at UNLV. Sandra had known the first moment she saw him in history class that he was the one, and every night with him was as exciting as their first. For Valentine's Day he gave her an antique music box gift wrapped in poems he had written about her, and for her birthday his grandmother's engagement ring. Then one night he didn't show up for a date. No sign of him for the next three days as he didn't go home or to class. Sandra was scared sick, until on the way back from checking with the campus police she saw him at the student union. He looked her in the eye, then turned and walked away. She followed, straight into a cold shoulder. Was devastated. Could not understand what she might have done to make him act this way. Did he have a new girl? Whatever it was, she was at least owed an explanation. For days she pursued him, crazy with confusion as he refused to even speak to her. Then he was gone. From school. From his apartment. From her life. And now twenty years later she had him cornered on a downtown bus. She sat down and demanded that explanation.

Bob picked jam from the big toe that protruded through a hole in his sneaker, then reached into his pocket and showed off half a dozen coupon books he had recycled from various trash cans. Free nickels. Free hot dog. Free spin. The bus passed Paris, then Bally's. He told her about the pancakes at the El Cortez, about his imaginary brother and the doorways where he slept. But not a word about what happened twenty years ago.

After the breakup Sandra quit school and rebounded into several brief relationships, sabotaging each one by holding the victim up to the impossible standard of what had once been. She became bitter and alone. Blamed Bob for all that was lacking in her life. Bonded with similarly resentful women whose misfortunes were canonized on the Lifetime cable channel, allowing Sandra to grow content in her own bitterness. A bitterness so consuming that it was the only emotion she allowed herself to own. She often dreamed of running into Bob and making him jealous while on the arm of some handsome millionaire at the hottest nightclub or snootiest new restaurant. But sadly, most of her forays into the night consisted of listening to jazz fusion at some brewpub, her self-esteem evaporating with each number as she watched men older than herself hit on women younger. She looked at Bob, all of a sudden feeling better about herself through his misfortune.

The bus passed the Flamingo, the Venetian. Then Bob blurted out the name Scott Post. A college classmate who had been hot for Sandra, but whose pitch always sailed outside the strike zone as she was in love with Bob Brewer. The same Bob Brewer who now sat beside her on a downtown bus, sucking pus from an open sore on his arm.

"What about Scott Post?"

"You were fucking him behind my back."

"Are you insane?" For an instant she regretted her choice of words, but only an instant as she was now as angry as she was confused.

"I saw him at your apartment."

"He was *never* at my apartment!"

Bob looked out the window. The Riviera. The Sahara. "When I came over to pick you up that night, Scott Post's car was parked in front of your building."

Sandra denied it, then stopped on a dime as two and two all of a sudden made four. "Oh God. Bob, he just stopped by to return my English Lit notes. He didn't stay long enough to sit down."

But in Bob's mind he had. In Bob's mind, Scott Post had been inside fucking his girlfriend on the same bed where he slept. On the same couch where he watched television. On the same kitchen table where he ate his Cheerios. Bob got drunk. Stayed drunk. Whatever it took to keep a focused vision of Sandra with Scott Post from ever again entering his head.

Sandra's heart sank. How could a man who professed unconditional love be so stupid with jealousy that he ruined both their lives rather than simply asking for what was a logical explanation?

"Bridger Street," called the driver.

Sandra stood and looked at Bob. What if she cleaned him up? Got him a job? There was no reason she could not still embrace happiness as Mrs. Bob Brewer. She pulled a silver necklace from inside her dress and held the engagement ring that had rested over her heart for the past twenty years. Fate was allowing her the opportunity to right a terrible mistake and finally claim the love that was hers. But Sandra had long ago committed herself to an emotion far more intimate. Had become so invested in her bitterness that it was now part of her. A bitterness that had become as vital to her existence as the air she breathed. Love never stood a chance.

Sandra got off the bus, morning perspiration clinging to her floral print dress as she walked up Bridger toward a work day destined to be as monotonous as every other work day. Another rat in a maze sniffing the false promise of cheese.

The American Dream

"VIETNAM VETERAN." PROUD WORDS ON A SCRAP OF cardboard. Sad words as the sun-bleached letters had been traced over more than once. A sweat-stained regimental cap shaded the eyes of this man whose body had been shot in half two generations before, and who now toiled at the mercy of an unrelenting August sun that blistered the skin off the Las Vegas Strip. A plastic coin bucket wedged between the stumps of his legs begging help from the hordes of tourists that passed by during the course of his day. Some were generous. Some were cruel. Most just kept walking. Marty dropped a bill into the veteran's bucket.

Marty was thirty-five. On his way to meet friends at the Flamingo, but the heat was wearing him down so he ducked into the nearest casino for a quick beer. At the bar he caught sight of something far different from anything he had ever seen at a bar back home at four in the afternoon. Young and blond. Five-inch heels and a skin-tight mini-dress with high-beam headlights.

There were plenty of seats at the bar but Marty parked himself next to the girl. Found out her name was Jasmine. Bought her a drink and made the usual flatulent small talk. He was this. He was that. Owned this and owned that. Was in Las Vegas for some red carpet event.

"No, you're not." Jasmine gave him the once-over. Cheap watch. Golf shirt from some company tournament tucked into denim shorts. Five-and-dime sneakers. "You work in a cubicle. Drive a minivan. Your wife packs your lunch and mends your underwear. You play golf once a month on a public course and the only reason you got out of the house to come to Vegas is because you told her it was a convention and that your boss made you come."

"How much?"

"You couldn't afford it." Jasmine picked up her drink and moved to the other side of the bar.

Rejected by a girl who would have sex with anyone. That was some sucker punch to a man's pride. Still, Marty checked out her ass as she walked away. Then he turned three shades of angry as he saw the veteran's wheelchair parked at a $100 blackjack table. Watched in disbelief as the sidewalk beggar was betting strong and winning. Kept winning. Then lost twice in a row with 20 and saw that luck had switched allegiance to the other side of the table.

Marty slid off his barstool and followed as the veteran wheeled himself to the casino cage where he was met by a VIP host. Marty followed him onto an elevator. Exited on the 29th floor and watched as the veteran wheeled himself down the hall, then disappeared inside a corner room. Marty banged on the door.

"That was fast." The veteran opened up and looked at the man he did not recognize. "Sorry. I thought it was room service."

"You don't remember me?" Marty was not doing a good job of hiding his anger. "I gave you money outside."

"And you came all the way up here to get your dollar back?"

"It was a five."

The veteran looked at Marty's shirt. "Business must be good at Indiana Corn & Casualty."

"You think this is funny? What do you think all the other people who gave you money would say if they knew you used it to gamble?"

"After rent and groceries I do whatever I want with my money. I fought for that right."

A room service waiter arrived with a bottle of Jack Daniel's and a bucket of ice. They went inside and the veteran signed the check. Offered Marty a drink.

"I don't want your drink."

"Would you be this moralistic if I supplemented my disability check selling pencils, then went out to drink beer and play nickel slots?"

"The VA has programs to rehabilitate people like you into productive members of society."

"What do you know about people like me? Ever been inside a VA hospital? A thousand patients with a thousand different problems. Two doctors. Almost forty years ago they patched me up, gave me this chair and pushed me out into the street. There's more compassion at an HMO."

"Times have changed."

"The only thing changed is that today's returning soldiers are hailed as heroes. Back then we got spit at."

"Bitterness isn't going to get you anywhere."

"You got it backwards, pal." The veteran spun his chair toward the window and admired the spectacular view. "I'm living the American dream. Free to come and go as I please and enjoy anything the world has to offer. Plus, I just won $1,200."

"And tomorrow you'll lose it back, so what's the point? What do you get out of it?"

"A chance. Any time I have $5 on the pass line I have a chance to hold the dice for an hour and parlay that five into a house on the golf course."

"But you never have."

"But I might." The veteran poured himself a drink. "Which is more of a chance than you'll ever have, shackled forever to a job you hate just to pay the mortgage on a family who probably only knows your name when they want something. There's not a dime's difference between you and that lamp over there. You have no more freedom to come and go as you please than that lamp has to turn itself on and off."

"Don't stereotype me."

"You stereotyped me. The difference is that I'm right. Guys like you come to Las Vegas to do all the things you can't do at home. But you can't really afford it so you drink a little more than usual and work on the lies you're going to tell the guys back at the office on Monday."

There was a knock at the door. The veteran wheeled across the room and opened it. Young and blond. Five-inch heels and a skin-tight mini-dress with high-beam headlights. Jasmine sat on the bed and the veteran poured her a drink, then smiled at Marty. "I fought for freedom for both of us." He rubbed his hand up Jasmine's bare thigh. "The only difference is that you don't take advantage of it."

Marty tried to convince himself of all the ways the veteran was wrong. That he was the one living the American dream. That he liked the job that would require his on-the-dot presence another 7,140 times. That he liked the cramped house for which he was obligated to make another 317 monthly payments. That his family did know his name other than just every other Friday. But looking up Jasmine's dress as she made herself comfortable on the bed made it a tough sale. The more Marty thought about his life the more he began to see that it was nothing but a house of cards built upon a foundation of obligations. And that if he failed to live up to even one, his entire existence would come crashing down around him. Maybe it was true that there wasn't a dime's difference between himself and the lamp.

It became obvious that three was a crowd and Marty turned to leave. Said goodbye to the veteran but his eyes were on Jasmine. On her still as the door swung shut behind him. Waiting for the elevator, it hit Marty hard that he was indeed living in a fool's paradise. That his life back home was good only because he had thought it was good. That he had never known any different. He wished to God that he had never asked for his five dollars back.

Machine Gun Joey

Joe Effers had not confessed to killing those four people during the robbery at the restaurant, but with the evidence the police found stashed in his apartment he may as well have. An open-and-shut case. The kind of can't-win situation a high-profile mouthpiece like Stephen Collingwood took on pro bono to get his picture on the front page. Would prolong to keep his picture on the front page. And if by some miracle his courtroom theatrics managed to win his client an acquittal, the telephones at his office would ring off the hook with new business for a year.

Collingwood dressed expensively. His hair was white with experience and his voice retained a hint of magnolias, even though he had been defending murderers in Las Vegas for over twenty years. He grew frustrated as the prisoner in the orange jumpsuit offered no excuses. No alibi. Not one word in his own defense. Just sat across the table chain smoking. "Four people are dead. The district attorney is going to push hard for the death penalty if you're convicted."

Late thirties. Bushy brown hair and sunken cheeks. Joe wore a natural look of defeat, as if life had dealt to him from the bottom of the deck. He lit another cigarette. "The needle or the nicotine. Doesn't matter much to me either way."

"You have lung cancer?"

"Working on it."

"Who else was in on the robbery with you?"

"Nobody. Check the surveillance tape."

"So you admit you were there. Did you kill those people?"

"Sure. Why not? Like I said, it doesn't matter much to me either way."

"If you committed the crime alone, who turned you in?"

"Anonymous caller."

"Someone who knew that you worked at the convenience store across the street from the restaurant. Someone who knew that the ski mask you wore was in a bag stuffed under your kitchen sink." Collingwood leaned forward as if cross examining a witness he had on the ropes. "What was your motive?"

"Money."

"What was your motive to kill four innocent people who were lying helpless on the floor of that restaurant? None of them saw your face. You could have just walked out. The truth is you had no motive."

"It was money."

"You had a job. People who commit armed robberies blow the money on drugs or a good time. What did you spend it on? What was your motive?"

Joe put out his cigarette and lit another. "I remember driving with my dad one afternoon when I was five or six. He was taking me to get a haircut when all of a sudden a car started following us. My dad made a couple quick turns but they were still on our tail, so he punched the gas and squealed around corners until he finally lost them and hid the car behind the mortuary on Main Street. He grabbed me and we ran inside. There was nobody there so he lifted me inside a display casket, closed the lid, then took off. I laid there for hours scared to move, not knowing that my dad had been shot to death before he made it back to the car.

"For years I tried to block out the memory, but how is a kid supposed to forget lying in a closed coffin while his dad is outside full of holes? It didn't help that my mom played it up big for her friends, especially when they started making movies out of Vegas mob stories. *Big Maxie was in on the skim at the Stardust. Big Maxie was rubbed out because he knew too much.* But never a mention of Big Maxie's kid scared shitless inside that coffin."

Collingwood made notes on a legal pad.

"When I was twelve I went to the library to check out old newspapers to see what they said about the mobster who stuffed his kid in a coffin. The newspaper stories differed in degrees of sensationalism, but the facts were all the same. Maxwell Joseph Effers — there was no mention of the name Big Maxie — was a small-time crook who had been sent up twice for armed robbery. Nothing but a two-bit hood.

"When I told my mom what I learned at the library, she beat me bloody. Screamed that I was a liar and that I'd never be half the man Big Maxie was. That I didn't have the guts. Said getting pregnant with me cost her a spot in the Folies at the Trop. And those two minutes it took Maxie to stuff me into that coffin cost him his life and her a meal ticket. She hated me because she had to work nights to feed a kid rather than partying on the Strip. She gave me one of Maxie's guns and told me to either go rob somebody or shoot myself in the head. She didn't care which because she said I didn't have the guts to do either one. What a pair to draw to. A small-time crook for a father whose idea of good parenting was to seal his kid up in a coffin and a mother who wanted me to kill myself so she could go out dancing. I'm thirty-eight years old and don't remember what it's like not to have a headache. No wonder I have no friends. No wonder I ended up working graveyard at a convenience store."

Joe lit another cigarette. He felt good. It was the first time he had told that story to anyone.

Collingwood wrote a few more notes, then put down the legal pad. "What did you do with the gun?"

"Threw it in the lake."

"Why would you throw away the gun and not the ski mask?"

"I don't know."

"There's a no-questions-asked $50,000 reward for information leading to the arrest and conviction of the killer. Don't you find it odd that the anonymous caller who turned you in didn't try to claim it?"

"I guess. I don't know."

"You were the anonymous caller."

"I killed those four people."

"Your mother not only robbed you of the courage to live your life, she robbed you of the courage to shoot anyone, including yourself."

"I stood over those people and pulled the trigger four times! ME! JOE EFFERS!"

Collingwood put the legal pad in his briefcase. "You framed yourself to show your mother that you did have the guts to pull a trigger, and so she would see your name in headlines your father never got. And the bonus was that after it was over the state would put you out of your misery. But you made one mistake. You engaged a lawyer smart enough to see right through you. I could get these charges dismissed tomorrow, but I'm not going to. I'm going to turn this trial into a circus and the media is going to make me the most sought-after criminal attorney in the country when you're acquitted."

Joe Effers did get the attention he craved. In spades. But the press never lionized him with a colorful nickname like Big Joe or Machine Gun Joey. The slaughter was senseless and they portrayed him as a punk-ass coward. Then as Collingwood had guaranteed, he was acquitted. Proven gutless for his mother and all the world to see. Denied by a jury of his peers the escape of death that he was too cowardly to commit upon himself. He had nothing. Was nothing. Could no more climb back into the security of that coffin than he could climb back into the womb. There was nothing left for Joe Effers to do but go home and work on his three-pack-a-day cure for cancer.

Down at the End of Lonely Street

DENT-FACED STOOL JOCKEYS SUCKED DOWN ROTGUT IN A timeworn barroom stuffy with smoke and conditioned air. It was Las Vegas and the bars never closed, allowing these rummies the freedom to drink until they passed out and start again whenever they woke up. A routine Paul found enviable as he pounded vodka tonics to confuse the pain of being dumped by his girlfriend. Paul was not yet thirty. Sport shirt and slacks. Short hair spiked with products. A pampered son of privilege, slumming alone at this downtown dive rather than catching a buzz with his friends on their usual Friday night of ultra-lounging on the Strip.

Being dumped was the punch in the gut a man feels before realizing she did him a favor by opening the door for him to sleep with better-looking women. To explore new worlds of opportunity once he shook off the punch and stopped feeling sorry for himself. But Paul was just getting started. Alcohol didn't make him drunk in the traditional way. Just focused his anger. Fueled an inbred superiority as he watched bookend grandmothers drinking gin and smoking Luckies. Carbonated she-hens hanging onto backsore laborers with the ooze of a hard day's work still ripe on their clothes. A once-upon-a-time flower child in a tie-dyed dress dancing alone near a makeshift stage in the corner. Behind the bar a tight polyester shirt and symmetrically carved Afro branded the man in charge a refugee from the '70s. Though to Paul, he looked curiously futuristic flanked by yellowed photographs of forgotten sports heroes and the cheesecake model on a beer clock that had read 3:15 since Godzilla ate Tokyo. "Hey, Superfly! One more!"

Conversations hit the brakes as people who had spent their lives on the downside of advantage watched to see if the rich kid was going to get his ass kicked or just bounced into the street. Paul didn't care which. A black eye would be two steps up from the day he had had. But the bartender did what a good bartender does. Ignored him.

The wilted flower danced over to Paul. Her name was Penny. "I'll buy you that drink."

"I don't need you to buy me a drink."

"You do if you want to drink it here." Her voice was grainy from cigarettes. "You here to see Elvis?"

Who was this rusty old stove with the scraggly hair? He wondered if her pussy was as gray as her head, a thought mercifully ambushed by eye contact with a blonde at the other end of the bar. A streetworn tart with a store-bought rack stuffed into a cheap dress two sizes too small, and any other night Paul would have skewered her with the same contempt he was pissing on Penny. But this was not any other night. He was drunk, angry and alone. He would fuck this blonde in a New York minute. Fuck her until she hurt. Then fuck her again.

Penny interrupted his obvious thought. "When a guy comes in wearing a Rolex and he's not here to see the show, odds are it's girl trouble. Drowning his sorrows in the first dive bar that gets in his way."

Accepting a drink didn't obligate him to listen to barstool philosophy. Why couldn't this cankered old stove just leave him alone? Let him get his blood alcohol to a level where he would allow himself to wallow in the recycled poontang of the blond tart with the oversized rack.

Penny took a sip of her drink. "For something to begin, something has to end."

"That some Elvis lyric?"

"Opportunity." Opportunity Penny herself tossed away all those years ago when she had declared that no one would ever again have the chance to break her heart. And no one did because she never answered the door. When finally she was willing, nobody knocked. "When somebody breaks up with you, you can't waste time feeling sorry for yourself. You've got to look at the positive. Go out and meet new people."

"I can get laid anytime I need it."

"Of course you can." Penny looked as the blonde continued to flirt with Paul from the other end of the bar. "You're a man. You have money."

The room fell suddenly silent as the bartender pulled the plug on the jukebox. All eyes on a big man with black sideburns who stood center stage in a flared white jumpsuit and giant rhinestone belt buckle. He pressed the play button on the cassette player that would be his backup band. Struck the pose, then tore into "Heartbreak Hotel."

The room became electrified as oversized speakers detonated a voice that was surprisingly rich. Old ladies swooned and couples danced to the music that captured the spirit of a happier, more hopeful time. Even the dent-faced stool jockeys came alive as the man in the white jumpsuit revved this dive into a frenzy that made life briefly better for the weary souls who toiled eight days a week just to break even.

Paul didn't get it. Some fat guy singing in front of a tape player, yet if the real Elvis walked in nobody would give him a second look. Life's stepchildren who had every reason to be bitter at the hand they had been dealt, yet their feet tapped to the music as if they hadn't a care in the world. How could people with such wretched lives seem so happy? As he watched Penny dance away from the bar all he could see was some old stove to whom opportunity had long since given the kiss-off. Not a woman granted immunity from her daily grind in a room that made her feel like she was part of something special. That *she* was something special. That this was the one night of the week she could go home and maybe feel that it was okay to be alone.

Paul still didn't get it, but a couple of hours in this bar that time had forgotten was all the wake-up call he needed to shake off the punch and quit feeling sorry for himself. To refuel his feeling of superiority. Fate had dealt him all the aces and he had a lifetime to enjoy all his money could buy him, provided he break for the door before his foot started to tap to whatever it was that was so contagious in this geriatric gin mill. He disappeared into the night, toward the neon glitz of the Strip where he would catch up with his friends.

When the morning light would tap dance on Penny's head, it would be a hangover easily soothed by one part aspirin and two parts afterglow. She would think of Paul. She would feel sorry for him.

Parallel Lines

OSCAR DID NOT USE DRUGS. NEVER HAD. AND JUST AS HE WAS certain the occasional beer after work would not make him an alcoholic, he knew that the gram of cocaine he held in his hand would not make him an addict. Oscar was supposed to have been at work hours ago, the first time in two years he hadn't punched the clock at least five minutes early. Promptness looked good to the boss. Showed initiative. Initiative was the key to advancement. Advancement was the key to more money. More money was the key to the American dream of owning your own home. Something he and his wife could never have made happen in San Francisco, which was why they had crammed their lives into a third-hand pickup and aimed it south toward the promised land. Where the cost of living was manageable and jobs were available for anyone willing. Where, with the whacked-out real estate market, row upon row of beige stucco fronting three bedrooms and a pool was still affordable to even an unskilled laborer with a modest down payment.

The streets of Las Vegas were paved with gold. But for Oscar that was two years past tense. Today beige stucco fronting three bedrooms and a pool was the dream within somebody else's grasp, as Oscar's wife had left him and he knew for a fact that she was not coming back. He sat alone in the tidy apartment they had shared. Blinds drawn. The glint of morning sun sneaking between the slats his only clue that he had been sitting there all night. He tried to think of happier times but his pain wouldn't allow it. All he had was a bag of dope. Did they call cocaine dope? How the hell would he know?

Oscar leaned forward on the couch and popped the seal on a small plastic bag, emptying the white powder onto the glass-topped coffee table. Began to chop it with a single-edge razor blade. Knew the routine from the movies. He chopped slowly, then slower still as he was distracted by a framed collage of photographs that took him back to a happier time when he and his wife had first met. Eleventh grade. They rode the same bus home from school and every day for weeks he sat in the seat behind her. Close enough to smell the straight raven hair that tickled her shoulders. Drink in her infectious laugh. Each afternoon confident that this would be the day he would summon the courage to speak to her. Oscar had never been shy around girls before, but somehow this was different. When he finally did find his nerve, he stepped all over the smooth line he had practiced so many mornings in front of the mirror. He was mortified. But she quickly broke the tension with the kind of smile that lets a guy off the hook. Gives him back his dignity almost before he realizes he had lost it.

From that day on they sat together on the bus. Senior year brought intimacy, and the summer after graduation they were married, sharing the dream of a comfortable home with kids playing in the yard. But similar upbringing had made them both sharply aware that theirs was a dream they probably could never own if they had those kids before they could afford them. So they went to work. Long hours. Overtime whenever they could get it. But slinging pancakes at Denny's and stocking shelves at Costco were not enough to outrun the high cost of Bay Area living. For six years they pushed a rock up that hill, fueled by purpose and content with the pleasure they found in each other as long as there was enough left over on payday to rent a couple of movies and order a pizza. Oscar was one with his wife. She was one with him. Was.

Oscar's soul was now empty of purpose as he focused on his grief rather than the good times they had shared. Especially since the move. Even saving for a house they were able to afford to go out a couple of nights a week as locals casinos were ripe with food and drink specials. Affordable entertainment. Las Vegas had been very good to them until the dream was shattered. What good were three bedrooms if two didn't have bunkbeds? What was the point of growing old if you had to suffer it alone? Oscar took a deep breath and leaned back on the couch, finally rhyming a thought with reality as he realized that grief had made him selfish. She hadn't stepped in front of that truck on purpose. Feel sorry for her. She was the one never coming back. He still had his entire life in front of him. It was no consolation.

Oscar stretched across the table and unscrewed the top of a brass urn. Reached inside and pulled out a pinch of gray ash between his fingers and thumb. Sprinkled it onto the glass. Blended it together with the cocaine, scraping the blade to form the powdery ash into fat parallel lines. Rolled up a dollar bill. In the movies it was always a hundred, but this was hardly the movies. He placed one end of the rolled bill in his nose, leaned over the table and breathed in. Jerked his head back as the drug stung his brain. His pain was momentarily confused and he found himself surprisingly focused, his mind flashing back to the day she had first smiled at him on the bus. Their courtship and marriage. Pizza and videos at that first studio apartment they had called their own.

Remembered all the good times. Oscar snorted the second line and, until the buzz wore off, he would again be one with his wife.

Beautiful Stranger

SHE WASN'T THE BEST-LOOKING HOOKER IN LAS VEGAS, that's for sure. Past forty and every mile of it showed as extravagant makeup proved no defense against puffy eyes and the deep lines that bracketed her mouth. Curled brown hair was sprayed into place and clinging red slutwear shouted attention to the gravitational effects of age, which most women dressed to conceal. Why would a woman continue to prostitute herself into her middle years? Was she short on rent? Could she possibly have thought she was still hot? As long as men paid to have sex with her, why wouldn't she think she was hot? Although it was no coincidence that at the early hour of six p.m. there was no professional competition at the casino bar.

She caught the eye of a man checking her out. Picked up her drink and moved to the stool next to him. He wore glasses and was gray at the temples. A new sport shirt still creased from the store and tucked into khaki slacks made him look like any other middle-aged married man on the make who didn't know what the hell he was doing.

"I'm Candy."

"Steven." He shook her hand.

A prize sucker in a town littered with them, thought the bartender, grimacing in disbelief that some yokel would fork over hard-earned cash to stick his dick in this prune Danish when he could just as easily have a cherry tart. But Steven didn't see what a jaded Las Vegas bartender saw. He saw Candy as friendly. Beautiful. A sexy woman the likes of which he had never before touched.

Candy followed Steven's eyes on a slow scrutinizing journey down the length of her body. Eager eyes that did not hesitate at the imperfections. Eyes that told her that this man's fantasy was not to have anonymous sex with a gorgeous twenty-year-old girl. That this trick wanted a woman. A woman who would convince him that she went to his room because she liked him. That the money was just a gift. Maybe there was a market for middle-aged hookers.

Candy engaged him in conversation. Laughed at his jokes. Pretended to blush as she caught Steven checking out her pronounced cleavage. "Are you staying here at the hotel?"

Steven nodded, his heart rate amping up a notch.

"Mind if I see your room key?"

There was no time in a man's life more exciting than the moments leading up to sex with a beautiful stranger. A vixen in a clinging red dress who would soon make Steven's every sexual fantasy come true. He reached into his trouser pocket and pulled out a roll of bills. Folded inside was his plastic room key. He showed it to Candy.

She leaned closer and whispered, "Are you a cop?"

"What? Of course not."

"Do you have a plane ticket?"

"In my room. But I don't understand . . ."

"Relax, baby." Her smile put him at ease. Her hand on his thigh put him into orbit. "Just questions we girls have to ask."

He still had the roll of bills in his hand. "How much is . . ."

"Put the money back in your pocket. We'll talk about it upstairs." She noticed him twisting his wedding ring, then quickly stepped in front of any second thoughts. "Dating a working girl isn't cheating, Steven. If you come back to Vegas and call a girl other than me, that's cheating. Understand?"

Sure he understood, but only because he was getting hard watching her say it. He tipped the bartender and they disappeared into the casino. Steven was excited as they waited for the elevator. Candy knew it. Candy liked it. The elevator door opened and they stepped aside to let out two old ladies hell-bent for nickels, then a hotel security guard blocked their path. "Come with me."

"What for?" Steven pulled out his key. "We're going up to our room."

The guard was a recently retired Marine. New to hotel work. Overly fit with a shaved head that made his face look like a par-boiled ham. He put his hand on his gun. "Don't let's do this the hard way."

No one said a word until the three of them were out of the casino and into a fluorescently lit hallway somewhere in the nether-regions of the hotel. The guard took a Polaroid of Candy, then aimed the camera at Steven. "Your turn, pal. Metro started arresting johns, figuring when the wife sees your name in the paper you'll stay home like you're supposed to."

"This *is* my wife."

"Ya rent 'em, pal. You don't buy 'em."

Steven grimaced as his picture was taken, then took a deep breath and tried calmly to explain. "This *is* my wife. We're registered guests of this hotel."

"You're registered. The hooker isn't. Now let's see some I.D."

"That will prove we're married. Look at our licenses." Steven reached for his wallet.

The guard grabbed his arm. "Slow."

Steven handed him the license.

"Now you."

Candy produced her license.

The guard glanced at both, then made photo copies. "The last names aren't the same."

"Look at the addresses. The addresses are the same."

"Inside." The guard put Steven into a detention room and closed the door, then ushered Candy into the room next to it. "Move it along, sweetheart. You know the drill."

She did not know the drill, but soon would. She was given a card stating that if she ever again set foot onto hotel property she would be arrested for trespassing. She was being held for Metro Police who would formally arrest her for solicitation, then take her to jail. She sat alone. Scared. All because she and her husband wanted to add a little spice to their marriage of nineteen years. Role playing, that's all it was. Dressed like a hooker and calling herself Candy, she would pick up her husband as if they were strangers. It had the afternoon talk show seal of approval, so why not? What could go wrong? A sixteen-year-old daughter who expected her parents home by eleven, that's what could go wrong.

In the other room Steven paced, at the mercy of an overzealous security guard who probably would turn them over to the police even if he did believe their story. Which meant that even though they were innocent, by morning he and his wife would be social pariahs held up for ridicule by neighbors, relatives and the PTA. Steven was an insurance executive with a very conservative company. What would he tell his boss? That his marriage had become routine and Oprah said it was okay to dress his wife up like a whore and plant her at a casino bar? Would Oprah get him a new job? Put his daughter through college? A daughter who would quickly become the brunt of cruel jokes.

The role playing had been his wife's idea, but Steven could have said no. As head of the house it was his responsibility to play devil's advocate and look two steps ahead of anything for potential consequences. That's how he always explained things to his daughter whenever he had to tell her no. But when it came time to tell himself no, all he could think about was getting his rocks off. He had let his family down. Humiliated them in exchange for a few hours away from the routine that was his life. But right now Steven would give anything in the world to get back to that boring routine of the suburban ghetto where the homeowners association would not let him paint the mailbox, the dog shit on the carpet and his teenage daughter played her music too loud.

The guard opened the door. "On your feet."

Steven's stomach was queasy and his new shirt was ringed with cold sweat. This was it. Life as his family knew it would never be the same. He and his wife stood in the corridor before the two Metro officers who would take them to jail. Steven gave it one last shot. "Please believe me, officers. This is not what it looks like. She and I are married."

The security guard winked at the policemen. "That story gets funnier every time he tells it."

"We ARE married!" Steven raised his voice, knowing at this point that anger could not possibly make the situation any worse. "This idiot has copies of our licenses which prove it."

The policeman in charge asked to see the copies of the licenses and the guard handed them over. He checked the addresses, then crumpled the copies and tossed them into the trash. Looked at Steven. "We apologize for the mistake. You're both free to go."

The guard cursed the air blue.

"Does she look like a hooker who could make any money around here?" The policeman was angry. "Next time make sure you actually have something before calling us off the street."

The insult sailed over their heads as all Steven and his wife heard were the words *free to go*. They found their way back through the maze of corridors to the casino. Approached the exit where the valet would fetch the getaway car that would take them back to their suburban house with the beige mailbox, dog shit on the floor and teenage daughter who played her music too loud.

Steven stopped and leaned against a slot machine. The ordeal had left him shaken. "I need a drink."

His wife smiled seductively. Caressed his cheek. It was no longer scripted spontaneity as she reached into his pocket and pulled out the room key, then whispered in his ear, "There's a mini-bar upstairs."

Steven looked at his wife. No longer as the beautiful stranger, but as the soul mate who had been put on this earth just for him. Like new lovers, they raced for the elevator.

Peace

DANNY'S SHIRT WAS DAMP WITH SWEAT AS HE SAT IN A creaky straw-bottom chair, counting to see who had the most chips in a hanging velvet tapestry of Jesus shooting crap with Elvis. He gazed out the window of the trailer as late-afternoon sun bleached the sterile emptiness of rock and sand, his eye catching on a lone spindly weed. A prickly blemish the tree huggers probably had christened with some resplendent botanical name. The more he looked, the more he could not see the beauty that so many seemed to find in the weary nothingness of the desert. He glanced at his watch, then blew a smoke ring as if he hadn't a care in the world. And soon he would not. Because Danny knew that in exactly eight minutes he would be dead.

Playing poker in the kitchen was a nasty-looking whore, naked except for a cast on her leg. She was thirty. Looked forty. The blistering heat fermenting her ripeness. To her left sat a drunken Indian, and across the table a pencil-neck kiddie fucker with the unmistakable outline of a switchblade bulging the back pocket of his jeans. The condemned man shook his head at the awkward sleight of hand as the kiddie fucker filled a spade flush from the bottom of the deck. Would he be the one? If he wielded his knife with the same ineptness as he manipulated the cards, death was certain to be slow and painful. Piercing steel in his gut a lightning rod for pain so intense he was unwilling to imagine it.

It was not that Danny was afraid to die. He just didn't want to. Twenty thousand tomorrows of missed opportunity. Would it be the Indian who had, up the road on the Paiute Reservation, gunned down his own brother for drinking his last beer? Maybe they would force Danny to give the one-legged skank a quick what-for. That would certainly kill any man one way or another. And one way or another it would be. At the hand of some insult to evolution who couldn't cash a show ticket in a three-horse race. Then Danny paused his thought, stung by the unprejudiced epiphany one feels as the inevitable rounds the far turn into the stretch. Realized that he had no foundation to judge himself superior. What had he accomplished in his thirty-two years that was so noble or important? Dealt five-dollar blackjack? Worked on his tan? Chased girls after work? It wasn't much for which to aspire.

At exactly five o'clock a craggy-faced man with long white hair will push open the door of the trailer. Without a word he will turn to Danny. Stare at him for that longest of moments, then relax his facial muscles into a thin smile. Lecherous bloodlust will quicken his pulse. He will nod to the poker players. One will stand.

The condemned man's mind will explode in an urgent kaleidoscope of emotion. Should he make a run for the door? Even if he made the door, how far would he get? Where was the girl who had suckered him into this corner? Easy money, she had said. Not really stealing if you rob criminals, she had said. Desert rats who were always stoned out of their minds, she had said. In and out before they would know what hit them, she had said. It was a simple robbery, what could go wrong? Yet it had gone wrong. Terribly wrong. With a spot of luck the girl had made good her escape. But for every winner there is a loser.

Other than a streak of healthy larceny, Danny had never done anything blatantly dishonest in his life. Yet there he sat. Caught, convicted and sentenced to die in the blink of a moment by the white-haired Svengali to a savage cult that had little in common except a taste for peyote. A maniac who had lurked unnoticed in the desert for twenty years. Hijacking displaced people with no direction. Dispatching the converted into Las Vegas to rob prostitutes and abduct them back to the trailer for ritualistic sexual torture. Then death. All of which Danny had learned after the fact. Too late to have given his brain veto power over his dick. Now going the inevitable route of every man who thinks with his dick. Only he was on the express. Three minutes to the end of the line.

Danny had thrown his hands in the air at the sound of the shotgun blast. She never broke stride. The car, his car, kicking up rock and dust as she sped off in the direction of the highway. His urgent call to her voicemail saying they would let him go if she returned the stolen cash box, but that he would be murdered at the stroke of five o'clock if she didn't. What if she didn't get the message? What if she did? He hardly knew her. Just some piece of trim he had picked up at the casino bar after his shift a couple of nights before. A stranger. A great blow job with no last name. A girl who was now safe in Las Vegas with a bankroll. Why would she return it to a maniac who would undoubtedly kill them both even if she did?

Where would Danny be if he had gone to college? Should he have been kinder to his mother? Helped the less fortunate? He never met his true love. Never saw Paris or read *Moby Dick*. What if there really was a god? Too much too quickly for the human brain to compute. The clock was ticking. Seconds before five o'clock. Overwhelmed by a blitz of hindsight and regret, the chaos inside his head denied him clear perspective. His thought process began to shut down. He looked out the window and saw the lone spindly weed standing defiant against the assault of late-afternoon sun that scorched the sterile emptiness of rock and sand. A landscape still displeasing to his eye, yet he could not look away. Somehow drawn to the vast nothingness of the desert and, to his surprise, discovering that the pain of his anticipation was soothed by a certain vacuous serenity.

Danny rested his sweat-soaked shirt against the back of the creaky straw-bottom chair. Casually blew a smoke ring. Mind uncluttered. He would have one final moment of peace. Then he would be dead.

Acknowledgments

SPECIAL THANKS TO CAROL CALDWELL FOR ENCOURAGING me to keep pushing the rock up the hill. To Geoff Schumacher and Carolyn Hayes Uber for validating my vision. To Jessie Pound for her unwavering commitment. To Dayvid Figler for pointing me in the right direction. To Jarret Keene for being in the right place at the right time. To Gregory Crosby, Geoff Carter and Andrew Kiraly. To all the great fiction writers who inspired me to do well, and all the bad fiction writers whose undeserving works pissed me off enough to do better.

About the Author

P Moss, a writer, gambler and bar owner, has been at Las Vegas' cultural forefront for almost twenty years. He grew up in the Midwest and studied journalism at the University of Minnesota. Shortly after, he moved west, drawn to the gambling action of Las Vegas. He went on to live in New York City and Los Angeles, but always desired to return to Las Vegas. In 1992 he did return and created a bar reflecting his unique style and personality, the world-renowned Double Down Saloon. In 2006, Moss opened a second Double Down Saloon in New York City. He recently launched the Polynesian-themed Frankie's Tiki Room in Las Vegas. *Blue Vegas* is his first book.